BLUE
GLASS

BLUE GLASS

GLASS

SANDRA TYLER

A HARVEST BOOK

HARCOURT BRACE & COMPANY

San Diego   New York   London

Copyright © 1992 by Sandra Tyler

Library of Congress Cataloging-in-Publication Data
Tyler, Sandra.
Blue glass/Sandra Tyler.—1st ed.
p.   cm.
I. Title.
PS3570.Y527B5   1992
813'.54—dc20   91-30720

Designed by Trina Stahl

Printed in the United States of America

First Harvest edition 1993

A B C D E

To my mother and father, always,
for their enduring love and encouragement, and
for the integrity of their own visions

And to Evelyn Horowitz,
for all her insights as a
teacher and friend

BLUE GLASS

ONE

We were driving up to Aunt Holly's summer house on Indian Lake, a trip we made every July. Aunt Holly was my mother's only sister. They had "never been close," as my mother would explain—on her birthday she would carefully repack into their boxes Aunt Holly's gifts of Disneyland beach towels or Hot Stuff aprons and save them for the church fairs. My mother always gave Aunt Holly the same thing for her birthday, bath oil balls and scented soaps in the shape of hearts.

"I don't know why we can't make a picnic of it, Dale," said my mother, rolling up her window an inch. She rolled it down again; she didn't want her hair to blow out of her kerchief but the air conditioning didn't work.

"There's no place to stop, Marion," said my father, who did all the driving. My mother was afraid of traffic.

"There's a grassy stretch all along here," she said.

"Wouldn't you just like to get there?"

"Let's get there, let's get there," I chanted, hanging over the front seat. I was excited about seeing my three cousins, about once again becoming absorbed into their family that felt so much bigger than my own. The only other time I saw them was at Christmas when we all met at my grandparents'.

My mother looked at me, the sun filtering milkily through her blue mascara. She turned to stare at the thin line of bushes dividing the highway. "Well, it just seems a shame. I was up at dawn, baking that chicken, trying to prepare a nice lunch—"

"We'll have your picnic." My father abruptly switched lanes and drew up on the shoulder of the highway.

"You'll like the way I made it," said my mother, fingering a button on her blouse. "It's a new recipe. Lemon chicken."

My father rolled his eyes. We got out of the car.

She pushed aside a few crushed Coke cans and spread out a yellow-checkered tablecloth that matched the quilted lining of the picnic basket. Kneeling, she handed us each a checkered plate and cup. The sun glinted off an abandoned hubcap. I picked up a cellophane wrapper that still held the shape of a cigarette box.

"You don't need to touch that," sang my mother. The heat and exhaust fumes didn't seem to bother her as she unloaded numerous containers of fruit and salad. She was as fond of making a production out of meals as she was out of doing laundry; in warm weather she washed our clothes in my old plastic wading pool on the patio, using the machine only for sheets and towels. My father looked at his watch as he did every night at dinner. I bent back my plastic spoon until I thought it would break.

Last, she pulled out the chicken wrapped tightly in aluminum foil. The cloth was cluttered with food as if we were expecting company. "There now." She leaned back on her heels. "Isn't this pleasant?"

"Lovely," said my father, wiping his face on a yellow paper napkin.

"I'm sorry," she said, pouring lemonade into our cups. "I'm being silly." Then she dipped her fingers into one of the cups and flicked them at my father. "But isn't this just a little fun?"

"We're on an *expressway*," said my father, but he was almost laughing now, taking off his spattered glasses to clean them.

"Feel that? There's even a breeze. We could be on

top of some breezy cool mountain, looking out over wild wandering fields, couldn't we, Leslie?"

"I bet there are even bears," I said, becoming caught up in her fantasy as, at ten, I sometimes still could in the stories she told me about the elves that had always lived beneath the bushes in our backyard.

"Bears, huh," said my father, reaching for a chicken leg.

My mother watched him as he bit into it. "So is it terrible?"

He nodded, trying not to smile. He leaned over to kiss her. "Just terrible."

She flicked an ant off the cloth, saying, "Well, you'll like the potato salad too."

When my father was full, he took off his glasses and leaned back against the car, closing his eyes. His face always seemed surprisingly soft without the square frames that so much heightened the squareness of his cheekbones and chin. My mother hoped I was inheriting his "strong features."

With his hand resting on my mother's knee, he dozed off, seeming to have forgotten about wanting to "just get there." Quietly my mother pulled out a sandwich bag of birdseed from the bottom of the basket. Usually she carried it in her purse for when we stopped at the park on the way home from school. We fed the birds in our backyard as well, and had trained the chickadees to peck from our hands. My mother believed that God "delighted" in the bird more than in any other creature. Otherwise He wouldn't have blessed it with what she thought to be the greatest gift of all, the gift of flight. And a flock of finches rising in a cloud from a telephone wire was no less miraculous than the blind man in the Bible who regains his sight; miracles, she would tell me, don't have to be rare.

Sparrows began to flock along the edge of the cloth. Their tiny, quick movements fascinated me. The only time I was able to sit still was when I fed the birds with my mother.

My father shifted, putting on his glasses, and the sparrows scattered. "Let's get going."

I jumped up, remembering how much I wanted to swim in the lake with my cousins. When my mother didn't move, my father and I snapped the lids back onto the half-full containers. She stared at the now empty grass, all the sparrows having flown back into the bushes, and I wondered if she was praying.

THEIR HOUSE WAS built onto a thickly treed peninsula where only small patches of grass could grow. The rest of the ground was blanketed with slippery, cool pine needles. When we arrived, I immediately took off my shoes and ran ahead of my parents. Everyone was down by the water so they hadn't heard us. My cousins and a few kids from next door were swimming, throwing rings onto the tentacles of a red octopus float. Aunt Holly lay on the raft.

Uncle Ryan was sitting on the dock reading a newspaper. "Look who's here!" he exclaimed, tossing his paper into a blue speedboat I'd never seen before, next to the old green one. A large man, he heaved himself up the small sandy embankment. He was a lawyer but it was hard to imagine him as one; I knew how he liked to carry a Snoopy lunch box to work and wear orange ties. I was happy to see that he wore the same visor he'd worn the summer before, the clear red kind that flooded his face with rainbows. From its band hung his lucky fish hook. He was better at catching fish than cleaning them—I'd seen him slash a pike down its stomach while holding it at arm's length but the fish had still been flapping as its insides spilled out. He had called for my aunt, who came and chopped off its head.

My aunt swam the sidestroke leisurely back to shore. She looked like my mother, tall and hipless, stalklike, but carried herself heavily as if leading a parade. My mother moved more lightly, and would sometimes be mistaken for having been a ballet dancer. They had the same needle-straight black hair that glistened with gray like new tar, even though Aunt Holly wore hers cropped above her ears. They both had knobby elbows and wore their watches loosely like bracelets, my aunt's a waterproof one that looked like a compass. My mother's had a silver band and the face was as small as a dime. But while my aunt's eyes were a deep brown, my mother's were an olive-green. In the sun they shone like the golden light in aquariums.

"Leslie," boomed Aunt Holly, leaning over to put her hands on my shoulders. "How are you, kiddo?"

Her touch felt so different from my mother's it was hard to imagine them as sisters, once little girls together. A difference that wasn't necessarily better, only startling, like that first bite into a cinnamon gum ball. Feeling suddenly shy, I pointed to one of the big white lilies on her suit. "We've picked those."

She pinched my cheek. "You certainly have. And you like to swim right out into the middle of those pads, don't you?" Dripping, she hugged my mother, who then fanned her blouse. Aunt Holly laughed. "I thought you'd like a wet suit after that hot ride."

My mother smiled wanly.

"And how is this handsome man of yours?" Aunt Holly asked as she kissed my father. She stood on tiptoes even though they were the same height. "I'm waiting to see him the least bit out of shape."

Uncle Ryan frowned, drumming on his stomach. "She's dying for me to take after you, Dale."

My father looked pleased, throwing back his broad shoulders, thrusting his hands deep into his pockets; he jogged every afternoon around the track of the college where he taught English. But no matter how trim my father could look, there seemed always to be something slightly askew, a coffee stain on his pants or a tail of his shirt that had come untucked, things that could send my mother into a frenzy, like the dirty socks he'd drop by their bed or his washcloth he'd leave rumpled on the edge of the bathroom sink. "New boat?" he asked, nodding toward the dock.

"She is," said my uncle. "Five hundred horsepower. We're now one of the fastest boats on the lake. We should sell that old green one, but I'm pretty attached to her."

"She's a beauty," said my father. He admired all their boats, including the two Sunfish and the fiberglass canoe pulled up under a birch tree.

One by one my cousins came out of the water. Jack was now fifteen and he'd begun to look like my uncle, his legs short and stocky and his irises completely surrounded by white so that he seemed always to be staring. Meg was the older girl, fourteen. Her features had begun to sharpen into those of Aunt Holly and of my mother, her nose long, lips thin. Joanne was eleven, a year older than me and my favorite; we had always shared our own special games, like building houses out of birch bark for our miniature plastic horses.

For a moment they surrounded my mother as they

always had when they'd all been young enough for her
to surprise them with blinking yo-yos and water pistols.
I was proud of how they still seemed to adore her; she
had been the one who'd take us into town for the kids'
matinee on rainy days, and afterward she'd treat us to
ice cream and give us pennies for the gum ball machines.
She was the one who took us for long walks through
the woods, helping us to collect different leaves and
berries that later we'd make into collages. She'd pretend
with us, forgetting herself as she became a wild cheetah
who'd stalk us through those woods—she'd crawl
among the ferns while we hid giggling behind the trees,
quite taken by how stealthily she seemed to move. When
we'd arrive back at the house, she'd remember herself
and quickly disappear to "freshen up," to wash the dirt
off her knees.

"So what'd you bring us this time, Aunt Marion?"
Jack asked, slipping his arm through my mother's.

My mother laughed delightedly, patting his hand.
"You mean to tell me you're not all too old? Well then,"
she said, opening her purse and pulling out four boxes
of sparklers. "Maybe you can't ever really outgrow
these."

I still loved sparklers myself but I was embarrassed
that she'd bought them for Jack and Meg, who now
seemed so grown up—I couldn't imagine them running
around waving them like we used to. Even Joanne

seemed too old, now that she wore her hair parted on the side. I still wore mine, the same black as my mother's and aunt's, in two tight braids.

For a moment my cousins turned the boxes over in their hands as if they'd forgotten what they were, and my aunt laughed. "Sparklers? Goodness, Marion, you're still spoiling them."

I was grateful when Jack said, "These are *great*, Auntie, thanks. We can't wait until dark."

Joanne grabbed my hand and whispered breathlessly, "Go get your suit on. Go change so we can play Marco Polo."

I tugged on my mother's skirt, unable to change until she unpacked the one large suitcase we all shared. She cupped the back of my head as she did on crowded escalators at the mall. "We have to get the bag out of the car still," she said, "and put those leftover salads in the refrigerator."

THE HOUSE LEANED sideways and the porch dipped down like a ramp. Inside, the floors slanted so much all the pictures seemed to be hanging crooked. My aunt didn't mind that the couch had faded from our sitting on it in wet suits. White rings from perspiring glasses had bleached the coffee table, a barn board supported by two cement blocks. Last summer my mother had brought a set of ceramic coasters for my aunt. Unused, they were displayed now on the mantelpiece, propped up like dishes.

What I loved most about the house were its surprises—a donkey puppet from Mexico hung in the window. A life-size fishing boy, originally meant as a garden decoration, sat on a trunk by the stairs. My aunt had fitted a pair of kid's sneakers onto its feet after she chipped off the toes while sweeping. This year I noticed something new, a cow-shaped vase. Black-eyed Susans blossomed from its open mouth.

"Isn't that the ugliest thing?" my aunt asked when she saw me looking at it.

A copper bell hung around its neck. I rang it, grinning. "Yeah."

My mother, clutching the picnic basket, continued on into the kitchen. "I suppose you still have that awful toilet seat."

Aunt Holly laughed. "I'm afraid we do, Sis."

The toilet seat was last year's addition, something they'd bought on a trip to Texas. Baby rattlesnakes were embedded in its clear rim. My mother couldn't sit on it without covering it with toilet paper.

EVERY YEAR MY parents and I shared the annex off the living room. I would have loved to have slept with Joanne and Meg, but they shared a room upstairs that was so small you could hardly stand up under the eaves.

I counted the rocks that lined the single shelf above the dresser to make sure they were all there. They were ordinary rocks, the kind found in the lake, translucent wet, but chalky when dry. My mother saw me take a couple of them down. She smiled sadly. "Those poor old rocks. They'd be happier in the lake."

"No, they wouldn't," I said, juggling them.

My father looked out at the lake through one of the two windows. The curtains patterned with bears and deer fluttered in the breeze. "That's quite a boat they bought."

"It should be," said my mother. "I'm sure they spent enough on it." Grimacing, she dusted the shade of the driftwood lamp with a Kleenex. "It wouldn't hurt them to spend a little of that money fixing up this place."

My father shrugged. "It's a summer house."

"Well then, they could spend it on their house in Syracuse. I can't remember the last time she mentioned having that place painted."

My father stretched out on their bed and breathed deeply. "I love that smell."

My mother opened the suitcase. "Of mildew?"

"The smell of wood. Of being in the woods."

She leafed through our carefully folded T-shirts.

"Don't you like that woodsy smell?" my father asked, tugging on her blouse so that she had to sit on the bed. "Just a little bit?" He slid off her kerchief.

Her hair dropped suddenly, heavily, onto her shoulders. She let it fall completely across her face as she stared down at the bedspread. She then combed it back with her fingers, only to let it fall again, and I knew that he was making her feel beautiful. My father liked to tell me about the first time he ever saw my mother: she was sitting under a maple tree outside their high school. She was sitting just like that, her head bent over a book as she combed back her hair with her fingers.

I could hear my cousins playing in the water. In the lap of my jumper I'd made a basin for the rocks and I now rattled them noisily until my father looked up. "Daddy, ask Mommy to give me my suit, please."

He massaged her neck. "Mommy, give her her suit, please."

Reluctantly she withdrew from my father. "They're probably wondering what happened to us."

My father collapsed backward and put his hands behind his head. "Let them wonder, then."

"No . . ." said my mother uncertainly, taking out my suit. A huge sunflower was sewn onto its front. Wetting her fingers, she pressed out the wrinkles in its petals.

THAT NIGHT, JOANNE and I fixed the beans in the kitchen while Meg and Jack set the picnic table outside for dinner. Aunt Holly slid chunks of meat, onions and peppers onto skewers and my mother prepared the salad. They stood next to each other at the counter.

Aunt Holly asked how my grandparents were; they lived near the beach in Connecticut, and my mother and I were spending the summer there as we did every year. My father came out on weekends.

"Leslie and Dad are making their usual salt water aquarium," said my mother. "They can spend hours collecting things."

"Have you and Mother been going to the dump again?" asked Aunt Holly.

"We've found some pretty interesting antique chairs this year. Their legs just need tightening or they need new cushions. I can't believe some of the things people throw out. At the end of the summer we're going to have a yard sale, so we thought we'd try to sell them and make a little profit."

Aunt Holly laughed. "You and Mother do have your projects."

My mother rhythmically clicked her knife against the cutting board, slicing cucumbers. "You should see them more often."

My uncle came in then, wearing a barbecue mitt. "The shish kebab ready?"

Aunt Holly handed him the skewers on a plate. "Please try this time not to let the onions fall into the coals."

He saluted her and left the kitchen.

My mother continued. "Every summer, they complain more and more about how they're not getting to see their grandchildren grow up."

"*I'd* like to see Grandma and Grandpa," piped in Joanne.

Aunt Holly frowned. "You saw them at Christmas."

"That's the only time they see them," said my mother.

Aunt Holly sighed. "It's different, you know, for you. You live only a couple of hours away. Besides, I wouldn't be allowed to leave there without having each and every one of my kids baptized and confirmed."

My mother looked at me and smiled proudly. "Leslie's going to be confirmed next spring."

"Please, Marion."

My mother grew quiet, and I was reminded that she was the younger sister, if only by two years. She held up a slice of cucumber to the window to see if the light could pass through it. She did this at home to see whether she was slicing them thin enough.

Aunt Holly set a bag of corn in front of us. We had to leave the kitchen then to husk it outside.

WHEN WE WERE all seated at the picnic table, Aunt Holly raised her can of beer. "I'd like to propose a toast. To myself. I'm going back to school."

"She beat me to it," said Uncle Ryan. "Can I finish? She's been accepted into the masters program in art history at Syracuse."

"Bravo!" exclaimed my father, clinking his can with my aunt's. "Good for you."

My mother had poured her own beer into a wine-glass. She swirled it gently. "That's wonderful."

"I was wait-listed, so I just found out."

"What made you decide to go back?" my father asked.

"Well, the kids are finally at an age when I can have a little more freedom. We discussed it, and they didn't mind the idea. I'm only going part-time anyway."

Meg shrugged. "If she wants homework, fine."

My father laughed. "Well, I think that's terrific."

My mother stared out at the tip of the peninsula.

"Aunt Marion, do you still have the magic box?" Joanne asked.

The "magic box" had been a tackle box filled with finger puppets, and when we were small, every night my mother would put on shows for us before we went to sleep. "Well, yes, I guess I do," my mother answered. "Somewhere."

"Don't tell me you haven't outgrown those too," said Aunt Holly, pinching Joanne's cheek.

"I was just wondering," Joanne said, now sounding embarrassed.

"I remember those," said Meg. "You made all those puppets yourself." She laughed. "You'd ask us all to save our old gloves."

"Yes." My mother nodded, looking back toward the peninsula. "Yes, I did."

"She's always liked to make announcements," whispered my mother as she got into bed that night. She had draped a towel over the lamp so it wouldn't wake me. I'd heard my parents come in from where I lay on my cot.

"We were talking in the kitchen before dinner," my mother said. "I don't know why she couldn't have just told me then."

"It's worthy of being announced, I guess," my father said.

Something, a pinecone maybe, rolled softly down the roof.

"You would like me to go back to school, wouldn't you?"

"Can't I be happy for your sister without you feeling insecure about it?"

"You didn't have to go on so."

"Sorry, sorry, sorry," my father hissed.

"Shh, you'll wake Leslie." She reached under the towel to turn out the light. She spoke so quietly then, I had to hold my breath to hear. "I never even got my college degree. Don't you wish I'd at least gotten that?"

My father yawned. "If what you want to hear is, yes, I think you should go back to school, then yes, I do."

"I'm raising Leslie."

He rolled over. "Good night, Marion."

"And I'm loving you. I love you so much . . ."

I was wide awake now. I stared into the dark in a way I didn't like to. My father didn't say anything more. In a moment he was softly snoring.

My mother sat up on the edge of their bed. Against the window, against the sky's gray light mirrored off the lake, she became a black hole. I wasn't used to watching her so secretly and felt faintly embarrassed, as I had once when I walked in on her while she was checking her breasts in front of the bathroom mirror. Without blinking, barely breathing, she gently probed around her nipples. When she saw me, she grabbed a towel and clutched it against her chest. I felt she'd do something like that now if she knew how I watched her.

I was glad when she lay down again, slowly lowering her head back onto her pillow. I waited for her to move. When there was no sign that she was still awake, I fell asleep to the beat of the water pump under the house.

JOANNE AND MEG crouched beside each other in the woods arguing over a salamander they both claimed to have found under the same log. "It's mine," Joanne said.

"Don't be a baby," said Meg, daintily picking up the

salamander by the tail and dropping it into her coffee can.

"I'm not," said Joanne, bumping gently against Meg. Meg bumped her back. They continued to bump each other, absently trailing their fingers through the damp earth. They seemed to have grown close in a way that was new, and I made myself look away from them. My gaze fell into a distant pool of ferns. It was exactly like that, a pool, the green of their leaves translucent and watery in the sun. This thrilled me, but it felt strange to be thrilled by something so simple; it was too simple to point out to my cousins who had become lost in each other. I pretended to be an ape, roared, picked up their log and flung it aside.

BACK AT THE house, Meg didn't care about saving her salamanders so she gave them to us. Joanne and I pulled out the two old spaghetti pots from under the house and filled them with earth. It had begun to rain so we carried the pots to the porch. We sat on the top step where we could keep dry but also reach the patches of moss, twigs and rocks we needed.

"Meg's done it, you know," said Joanne.

"Done what?" I was busy setting up individual beds of moss.

"In the tree house." She brought up a single pine needle and twirled it between two fingers. "She's done it. With a boy."

In the shadows of my pot, the salamanders seemed ugly to me, their pale red stripes having deepened to a muddy brown. The air had grown cold from the rain and I wanted to go inside. "I'm done," I said, reaching for the plastic wrap. I stretched it tightly across the top of the pot, secured it with rubber bands and quickly poked holes through it with a pine needle.

"Me too, I guess," said Joanne, gazing dully at her salamanders. "You know they'll escape anyway. They always do."

We tucked the pots under the wicker porch chairs.

We went into the kitchen, where we'd heard my aunt talking, I assumed to my mother. Instead, she was talking to the mother of the kids who had been in the water when we arrived. They sat at the table drinking coffee. Joanne stood beside Aunt Holly and, leaning against her shoulder, passed her hand through the steam rising from her cup.

I noticed a third cup, still half full. "Where's Mom?" I asked.

"I think she's taking a nap," said my aunt, cocking her head quizzically as if she were trying to understand me.

I SAT ON the edge of my parents' bed. Without moving her arm which was draped across her eyes, my mother asked, "Did you have a nice walk?"

"It was all right." I lay down beside her. "Were you praying?"

She still didn't move. "Not really."

I lay close enough so I could feel her skin, damp and soft. "I wish it wasn't raining."

I was glad when she lifted her arm to put it around me. "I know," she sighed. "Though I guess it's nice, that sound of the rain on the roof."

She smelled vaguely of dough. I breathed her in, let her fill me as I did on nights when I couldn't sleep and she lightly drew butterflies across my stomach, butterflies with large wings. She would have thought the ferns were beautiful. She would have pointed them out herself.

It rained through the rest of the afternoon and into the evening. A brief, violent thunderstorm put the lights out. After dinner, Joanne, Jack and I sat on the living room floor making shapes on the ceiling with flashlights and spatulas. My father and Uncle Ryan sat on either end of the coffee table playing chess and smoking cigarettes. They were my uncle's cigarettes, which he smoked only when he had someone to share them.

Meg and Aunt Holly took turns holding a flashlight for each other as they polished their toenails. My mother leaned into a circle of candlelight, working a needlepoint cushion for one of the chairs she had found at the dump.

"I don't know when I'll have a chance to be this

leisurely again," said Aunt Holly, squinting at her toes. "Next summer, I'll probably be catching up on reading. I hope I can keep up."

My uncle patted her ankle. "You'll do it. I'll make sure you do it."

"Isn't he wonderful? Sometimes, *some*times he can be just so wonderful."

"I don't know how you can do it," said my mother. "Balance it all." She tugged her thread taut. "Adolescence is the worst period."

Aunt Holly spoke slowly, matter-of-factly, as she carefully wiped the tiny brush on the edge of the nail polish bottle. "Well, there's never been anything you've wanted to do, Marion."

My mother secured her needle into the cloth patterned with violets. "It's stopped raining. I think I'll go for a canoe ride."

"There's not a light on the lake, Marion," said my father evenly. "You don't want to go out now."

"I don't?" said my mother. "I suppose you too know me better than I know myself." She gazed steadily at him. "Don't you?"

He looked back down at the chess board.

My mother let the screen door slam behind her.

When my father started to get up, Aunt Holly held him down by his arm. "She's all right."

"I should go."

"Maybe that's just what you shouldn't do."

He looked at her.

"She still likes to have people worry about her."

My father stared at the door. "It's just so dark out."

"Why don't we all play a game of Hearts," said my uncle.

"I think I'll go sit out on the porch for a while," said my father.

"Well, I'll sit with you," said Aunt Holly. "I could use a little air at this point."

I usually loved to play Hearts, the way we all sat together around the long table, but my mother seemed to have been gone a long time. In the candlelight our shadows loomed across the floor and walls, and I felt as I did waking from bad dreams, when everything felt distorted. It must have felt that way to Meg too, because as she dealt the next round she asked my uncle, "You don't think she could get lost, do you, Dad?"

"Oh, have a little faith in your aunt," said Uncle Ryan.

Jack turned around on the bench to look out the window. "It really *is* dark out."

I felt so afraid then, I got up and ran to find my father.

I stopped just inside the screen door. I could hear my aunt and my father talking.

My father's voice wavered unfamiliarly. "She can get so upset over things . . ."

"It's how she is," said my aunt soothingly.

I walked outside, opening the door wide so that its springs would creak.

They sat close enough for my aunt to drape her arm along the back of my father's chair. Her fingers hung down, just missed touching his shoulder.

"I think we should go find Mommy," I said.

"She's fine, honey," said my aunt. Her foot rested against one of the spaghetti pots.

I ignored her and looked at my father. "Let's find Mom."

"We should." My father pulled himself up. He had been sitting slouched. The chair seemed surprisingly too big for him, as it sometimes still did for Jack. "I'll get the keys to the boat from your uncle."

"I'm coming with you," I said.

He rubbed my head. "You bet."

BOTH MY AUNT and uncle came down with us to the dock. My father wanted to take the old green boat because he was used to it.

"You sure you don't want me to take you?" my uncle asked.

My father smiled. "Don't you trust me?"

Uncle Ryan handed him a big, powerful flashlight. "You may need this."

"She's really all right," said my aunt.

No one answered her. She went back up to the house.

My uncle stayed on the dock a moment longer to watch us.

The only other time when I'd been out in the boat at night was on the Fourth of July. Then firecrackers had burst across the sky. There was no light now at all except for candles in a few windows and that reflective glow; sky and lake bled together so that I could believe the real trees were those wavering across the water.

"How far could she have gone?" my father asked. He knelt on the seat, one hand gripping the wheel, the other shining the flashlight across the lake.

I shivered, pulling my hands up into the sleeves of my sweatshirt. "She's okay," I said.

He stared into the ghostly beam as if I hadn't spoken, and I suddenly felt terribly alone. I felt her absence then like I'd never felt it before, not when I'd lose her in a store or among the greenhouses of her favorite nursery. It hadn't occurred to me that something might actually have happened to her. It wasn't even as if she had drowned, but had become loosened from our lives and absorbed into the damp air.

Then I saw the outline of the canoe, a single curved blade, near the shore. My mother waved her paddle at us. "She's there!" I screamed.

As we slowly approached her, my father called out, half relieved, half angrily, "How did you get so far out?"

The canoe rocked in our wake. "I don't know. I just

kept paddling. I didn't know I could lose sight of the house so easily, that peninsula."

"You don't even have a flashlight."

He told her to pull the canoe up onto shore and we'd get it in the morning. She laughed nervously as he helped her into the boat. "I thought I'd have to spend the night in that thing."

She sat next to me, in the double seat behind my father, and we motored slowly back to the house. Nobody spoke until my mother said, "It's beautiful out, isn't it?"

"Why did you have to do that?" asked my father quietly. "Why do you have to let your emotions run away with you?"

She fingered the fan of spray along the side of the boat.

WHEN WE WERE at the dock, my father put out his hands to help my mother out of the boat.

"I think I'll sit here a minute," said my mother, clearing her throat.

"Fine." He put out his hands to me.

I tucked mine into my life preserver. "In a minute."

He wiped his hands on his jeans, put them in his pockets, took them out again. He ran them through his hair so that it stood on end. "The flashlight's there."

I watched him walk back up to the house. I hadn't

thought he would actually leave us there, though there wasn't much else he could do. He faded into the trees and I strained to hear his footsteps. At the same time I welcomed the silence that now surrounded my mother and me, a silence softened by the small rock of the boat, the raindrops dripping from the birch trees and patting the water. As we sat so close together, I even welcomed the lake's darkness; it seemed to contain us like a large deep bowl.

"Tell me," asked my mother, "do you think I'm a fool?"

She looked at me so earnestly I had to look away. "Mom . . . that's stupid."

Her face relaxed. "Look," she said. A lightning bug landed on her leg. She cupped her hands around it. I cupped mine on top of hers so that it lit up both our palms.

We peered down at the lightning bug until we heard the screen door. It was my cousins. They ran down to us waving their sparklers so that they seemed to be scrawling pictures on the night.

TWO

Our summers at my grandparents' were largely predictable; mostly I'd hang around my mother and Gramma June, playing with the cookie cutters while they sorted through the kitchen cabinets, or swinging in the hammock while they transplanted forsythia bushes around the yard. If Grampa Cole got off work early, he'd take me to the shore where we'd net baby eels and minnows for our salt water aquariums.

But the year he retired, when I was eleven, he started raising chickens. Gramma June told us again and again about the day he returned from his daily walk to the post office with a crate of chicks. He'd ordered them from Iowa, through a catalogue.

One morning I was watching him from the kitchen window as he gathered the morning's eggs into my old yellow sand pail. A breeze lifted his white hair, uncovering his bald spot. He'd built the pen in a corner of the backyard where nothing would ever grow. When my grandmother heard that he'd ordered the chickens to be kept as pets, she claimed she'd always dreamed of putting a goldfish pond there.

"He doesn't remember anything anymore," said my grandmother, snapping open the garbage can and yanking out the paper bag.

"Everyone forgets things . . ." said my mother, holding up a plate and watching her reflection slide into the sudsy water.

"He used to take out the garbage every morning without fail. Now he won't remember anything he doesn't want to. I have to remind him about the lawn too. And even to clip his toenails. He lets them grow as long as a cat's claws." Gramma June let the screen door slam as she carried the garbage outside. "He just spends all his time with those chickens."

It was unusual to hear my grandmother complain so about Grampa Cole. I was more used to the way she'd tease him, gently plucking at his wispy hair or tickling him under his arm when he protested about having to wear a suit to church. Sitting at the kitchen table, I sifted through one of Gramma June's baskets filled with chipped porcelain thimbles, old refrigerator magnets, barrette bows, shriveled chestnuts. I used to save these like treasures and examine them at night with a flashlight under my blankets, but now sifting through the baskets had become only a ritual. Some of them had been around since my mother grew up in that house. My father had grown up in Connecticut too, but his parents had retired to San Diego, for which I knew my mother was grateful; she'd never thought they felt she was good enough for their son.

My mother shook her head. "Those chickens."

"You like the chickens," I said.

"I don't *dis*like the chickens." She spoke into the sink. "It just wasn't right for your grandfather to go and order them behind your grandmother's back. It wasn't right."

I'd caught my mother gazing at the chickens the way she gazed at her favorite bird, the shy quail that only occasionally emerged from the woods. But because my grandmother resented the chickens, so did my mother; they did everything together. Every Saturday morning they went to garage sales, returning home with milk pitchers and Chinese lanterns, things soon forgotten in the hall closet or resold at our own garage sales. In church, they both knelt praying long after the rest of us, their faces buried in their hands. But while they both embraced Christ, my mother's God was simpler than Gramma June's. For Gramma June, God revealed Himself through lessons from the Bible. My mother didn't make me read the Bible; her God revealed Himself through the seasons. She told me He grew out of the earth like the tulips that lined our driveway every spring.

"What a perfect day," said Gramma June, coming back inside. "The humidity's finally lifted." Her mood had changed so suddenly she appeared transformed. She seemed less plump than full figured, and even seemed younger with one gray curl falling coquettishly across her forehead. Her dress looked as smooth as if it had been ironed, and its big orange blossoms didn't seem quite so faded. "I just hope it stays like this for Holly."

At the mention of my aunt, my mother's eyes grew dull. Heart-framed pictures of them as children lined the bottom shelf of the living room bookcase. Aunt Holly grins unabashedly into the camera. My mother looks away, picking at a scab or poking a stick into the ground.

"Won't that be something? I can't believe she's actually coming. She's always been so full of excuses, especially now that she's gone back to school," said Gramma June.

I watched my mother's hand wipe quick small circles around the table, the sun reflecting like splintered glass off the diamond in her engagement ring.

"Maybe the kids will like it so much here, going to the beach, they'll talk Holly into bringing them back next summer."

My mother arched her back as if in pain. "May*be*."

It had been my mother who had finally talked Aunt Holly into coming, but I knew she'd only done it to please my grandmother.

"I've got to get Cole to clean out the grill. He's probably forgotten about that too."

"They're not coming for another week."

"We don't need to leave things to the last minute." My grandmother laughed. "That's not like you anyway, Marion, to leave things to the last minute."

My mother wrung out her Handiwipe, twisting it as thin as string.

Gramma June leaned on the table in front of me so that I was sheltered between her arms. I liked how she smelled of bubble gum. I used to sniff through her powders, soaps and shampoos until I realized it was her own special scent. "Leslie, I hope you never deprive your mother of seeing her grandchildren grow up the way Aunt Holly has deprived me." She absently dipped her hand into my basket, letting the objects spill out between her fingers like jewels. "She's never tried to make me happy like your mother makes me happy."

"No, Gramma."

She kissed my head. "I know you wouldn't, sweetie." She moved over to my mother and squeezed her shoulders. "You're my blessing, Marion."

My mother shook out the Handiwipe, draped it evenly over the faucet.

I found a jacks ball in the basket, a clear one with

specks of silver suspended inside. I held it up to the window. The world became stilled. I felt my hand holding the ball, my elbow supporting my hand. I felt my own presence so painfully a cold wind could have been blowing through my bones. I suddenly missed my father even though I would see him that weekend—he taught summer school back home in New Jersey. But when he was here, we didn't really spend time alone together anyway. He'd take me fishing and I'd grow bored watching him, standing there with the tide washing over our feet. He wouldn't notice as I moved away and sat up near the dunes where I could tie knots in the long grasses. He'd follow the gulls down the beach as they hovered over the schools of bluefish, the patches of water that seemed to boil. But I didn't mind being left behind; I knew he'd eventually come back for me.

Forcing myself to move, I dropped the ball back into the basket and got up from the table.

"And where are you off to?" my mother asked.

I handed her whatever brass buttons and beads from broken necklaces I'd found in the basket. She liked to sew the buttons onto thin elastics for bracelets and macramé the beads into her plant hangers. "Just outside."

As I left, I could hear her jingle the buttons and beads like change.

GRAMPA COLE HAD finished collecting the eggs. Now he was watching the chickens. It did take some getting used to, seeing my grandfather like this, crouching with his long legs folded under him like a grasshopper's; it was from him that my mother and aunt had inherited not only their long thin faces but also their lanky height. I remembered the way he had been past summers, when he'd still been working for the local newspaper. He had been the production manager there, and on slow days I was allowed to visit him, to cut up scrap galleys and run them through the waxer. He had seemed powerful to me then, leaning over the light tables, measuring the boards with his yardstick. Now he seemed only awkward.

They were not ordinary chickens. The black ones, their feathers shimmering with blue, were from China and the white ones with thick plumes from Turkey. Long feathers trailed off their feet so they seemed to be wearing big slippers. "I can't tell them apart," I said, pointing to a pair of brown hens, their feathers rimmed with black.

"Oh, but they're so different," Grampa Cole said, sounding hurt. "See that one? See how she's off on her own? She's like that, independent. A real loner. And that other one, she's the exact opposite, loves to be around me."

My mother came outside. "Leslie, we're going to the dump now, if you'd like to come."

I pulled out a loose feather from one of their feet and examined its pattern.

Going to the dump was my mother's and Gramma June's favorite thing. The porch was furnished with old wicker chairs they'd found there and refinished. It had always been my favorite thing to do too. Grimacing, my mother would let me bring home plastic dolls missing half their limbs. I didn't play with dolls as much anymore and the sea gulls scavenging in the pit swarmed like rats. "I don't think so," I said.

"Well, all right," she said, smiling and trying to hide her disappointment. One of the chickens was kicking up a cloud of dirt, and she asked, "Why do they do that, anyway?"

"She's taking a dust bath," said Grampa Cole.

"A dust bath?" My mother giggled. "Seems to defeat the purpose, doesn't it?"

Grampa Cole grinned. "Not if you're a chicken."

She gazed at the chickens for a moment longer, then said, "Dad, I think you forgot to take out the garbage again."

He knitted his thick brows. "I did, didn't I?" He looked up at her. "I'm sorry."

She curled her fingers through the pen's mesh. "It's okay, really. If you could just try to remember next time. It upsets her so."

When she had gone inside, Grampa Cole said, "Watch this." His face brightened as the tame chicken leapt into his palm.

THE DAY BEFORE they arrived, I helped my mother set up the cots for my cousins in her old room, where I slept. She'd left the room the way it looked her senior year in high school, the year she married. Her old dolls sat on the bookshelf, their painted eyes the translucent blue of shallow pools in their china heads. Propped on her bed was her oldest stuffed animal, a poodle, its neck long since broken. Aunt Holly hadn't married until after she'd graduated from college, but even before that she'd taken everything with her except a hockey stick.

When we had made the cots, my mother unscrewed the top of her bedpost and pulled out the key to her vanity drawer. She sat down to unlock the drawer where she kept old charm bracelets, poems she'd written in school, the cross necklace from her confirmation, a pressed rose from her first date with my father. I was so familiar with these things it was hard to imagine them having belonged to a past other than my own.

"I hope your aunt and Gramma June will get along all right," she said, browsing through the drawer as she sometimes would, and I knew she wasn't looking for anything in particular.

I sat on her bed flipping the poodle's neck. "It will be weird," I said, "not having Daddy here."

I watched her in the mirror and saw how worry now creased her forehead, and I was sorry I had said anything; my father had always served as a bridge be-

tween my mother and Aunt Holly. But Aunt Holly had
agreed to come only during the week, when there was
less traffic, even though it meant Uncle Ryan wouldn't
be able to come because he had to work. The long drive
from Syracuse had always been one of her "excuses."

"I know," my mother said, looking past me in the
mirror to a print of Degas' dancers hanging above her
bed. She got up to straighten it even though it wasn't
crooked.

IT WAS RAINING when they arrived. Joanne and I kissed
each other stiffly; we'd finally outgrown the special
games we used to share at Indian Lake.

Jack brought in their bags. Where his shirt was un-
buttoned, I noticed a dark curliness I didn't remember
from the previous summer at Indian Lake. I couldn't
believe he was the same boy who used to cry behind
their compost heap.

"My God." My grandmother raised her hand to her
heart at the sight of fifteen-year-old Meg. She had cut
her hair so short her scalp showed.

Meg grinned. "Don't you just love it?"

"Her beautiful hair," my mother sang sadly.

Grampa Cole sucked in his lips, forcing back a smile.
Aunt Holly winked at him. Her own hair wasn't very
much longer than Meg's.

"Dear God." Gramma June hesitantly touched Meg's
head.

"*Hello*, Mother," said Aunt Holly.

"How could you let her?"

"Mother, let us get in the door before you start on us."

"I'm sorry. Well, I'll just make tea then," said Gramma June, looking around as if she'd forgotten where the kitchen was.

AT THE BEACH, which was a couple of blocks from the house, Joanne and I drew roads in the sand with our palms. If we had been a few years younger, we would have built whole towns for our matchbox cars. Now she abandoned me, lost in her own private daydreams; she fingered her gold hoop earring secretly, her hand hidden beneath her hair. My mother wouldn't let me get my ears pierced until I was fifteen.

Jack came up from the water. His chest hairs seemed thicker as he stood in his own shadow. The back of my neck tingled as it sometimes did when I examined my math teacher while he wrote on the blackboard—he wore his pants so tight I could see the outline of his underwear. I dug my roads deeper so that they could pass through mountains.

Through purple sunglasses, Meg was watching two boys play paddleball. Jack shook his wet head over her so that she sat up with a squeal and chased him into the water.

"Do her girlfriends shave their heads too?" asked

my grandmother. She and my mother sat beneath the umbrella, both wearing long-sleeved shirts over their bathing suits. Towels were draped across their legs.

"Of course," said Aunt Holly, opening a bottle of suntan lotion that smelled of coconut. "Why else would she shave her own?"

"It's just not particularly becoming."

"She thinks it is. That's what counts. And everyone else thinks it is. That counts even more."

"If it were the style to wear a ring in her nose, would she do that too?"

"I would have at her age."

"I wouldn't have let you."

Aunt Holly watched a fish kite rise and fall above the waves. "I know you wouldn't have."

My grandmother wrapped her towel more tightly around her legs.

"So how's school?" asked my grandfather, shading his eyes. Gramma June had tried to get him to sit under the umbrella so that his bald spot wouldn't burn. He'd forgotten his hat.

"Oh, it's wonderful, Dad. Right now I'm studying the old ivory carvings of the Eskimos from northern Alaska. You'd be interested in that—you've always wanted to go to Alaska."

"I still do," said Grampa Cole. "The American bald eagle is there."

Meg was now playing paddleball with one of the

boys. Joanne retired from her roads and lay back on her towel. She tapped out a tune with her foot, singing quietly to herself.

"So what do you think you'll do with your degree?" asked my grandmother.

"What am I going to do with it? I'll go on for my Ph.D., I guess."

Grampa Cole smiled broadly. "A Ph.D. We've never had a *Ph.D.* in the family."

"What then does one do with a Ph.D.?"

"Mother, it's not necessarily a matter of what you *do* with it."

"You could teach," said my mother. "Like Dale."

"I don't know that I want to teach."

"Why not? Dale loves teaching."

"First of all, I'm not Dale. Secondly . . ." She threw up her hands. "Can't you two accept that I'm doing this maybe just for myself?"

"I'm proud of you," said my grandfather.

Aunt Holly squeezed his hand. "Thanks, Dad."

"I'm proud of her too, Cole," said Gramma June.

He stood up wearily. "I need to stretch my legs." He began walking slowly down the beach.

Gramma June raked the sand with her fingers. "There was a time when he would ask me to come along. When we took walks together."

"Retirement's an adjustment," said Aunt Holly.

"It's those chickens." Gramma June sighed, staring down the beach. "I'm just waiting for him to get tired of those chickens."

She sounded so sad then, I wondered if she was remembering how Grampa Cole would walk with his hand against the small of her back as if supporting her. They'd collect shells and occasional dried sea horses in Grampa Cole's hat. I followed Gramma June's gaze down the beach. He had paused to examine an abandoned sand castle.

THE NEXT DAY, Gramma June went shopping with Aunt Holly, who wanted to explore the latest boutiques. My mother told them to go along without her, that she didn't mind staying behind to tidy up the house. But she ended up playing Monopoly with me and my cousins on the porch. Grampa Cole had fallen asleep in one of the wicker chairs, his newspaper sliding off his lap. We could hear the dishwasher through the open kitchen door.

My grandfather folded his paper as if about to get up. "We've come to the dock," he announced.

We all looked at him.

"Didn't you hear it? The engine's stopped. It's time to get off."

"That's the dishwasher changing cycles, Grampa Cole," said Jack. "You were dreaming."

My grandfather wiped his mouth on the back of his

hand. He laughed embarrassedly. "Of course." He re-opened his paper. A moment later he asked, "So when will Mary be home?"

All the little sounds, a bird rustling in the hedge, the scratch of the chickens, the drip of last night's rain down the gutter, seemed suddenly sharpened, to echo metal-lically; Mary was his sister. She'd died of a burst appendix when Grampa Cole was seventeen.

My mother seemed about to say something and we waited for her to remind him about his sister. Instead, she picked up the dice and gently rolled them in her palm. "I don't know, Dad," she said, without looking at him. "I'm not sure exactly when she'll be home."

"I REMEMBER RUNNING through those woods," said Aunt Holly after dinner, staring into the trees lining the yard. She and my grandparents and mother were sitting around the porch table. Joanne and I roasted marsh-mallows.

"There was that path that led to that little clearing," my aunt continued. "And I used to pretend a spaceship had landed there. In the summer, I'd sneak out at just about this time, thinking they might come back."

"I used to worry so," said Gramma June. "You dis-appearing like that, just before dark. And all that poison ivy."

"I don't remember a path," said my mother.

"That's because you'd never come along, you were afraid to."

My mother picked a bread crumb off her lap.

I looked out at Jack where he swung in the hammock.

"See you all later," Meg said, sweeping past us. She'd changed into a long black shirt and black pants so tight they could have been stockings.

"Not too late!" Aunt Holly called after her.

"Where's she going?" asked Gramma June.

"To meet that boy in town she saw at the beach."

"You're letting her go off with someone she just met? He's not even picking her up?"

"Mother, he's perfectly harmless. And they're just going for ice cream."

"Well, it's not him I'm worried about," said Gramma June. "Look how she was dressed."

Grampa Cole abruptly pushed back his chair. "I'd better go lock up the chickens."

"I trust her," said Aunt Holly.

"She's just a child," said my mother.

Aunt Holly frowned. "You wait until Leslie's that age. Hopefully, she'll be as good as you always were."

I let my marshmallow drop into the coals so that I could watch it blacken and shrink to nothing.

"Marion *was* good," said Gramma June, patting my mother's knee. "Thank goodness, at least she never gave

43

me a day's worry. She didn't run off across the country with only a knapsack, never writing, or disappear with some strange boy into the mountains—"

"You know what I think, Mother?" said Aunt Holly. "I think I've always upset you and still upset you because you wish you'd done those things."

Gramma June stood up then, gathering the dishes.

Aunt Holly watched her carefully. "That's it, isn't it?"

The loose skin on my grandmother's upper arms began to shake. She quickly carried the plates inside.

It had grown so dark I could see only the white soles of Jack's sneakers. But I felt him there. I felt him there like a still pond whose surface I longed to break.

My mother collected the rest of the dishes. She handed me the breadboard and butter plate. "I don't know why you have to do this."

"I'm not doing anything, Marion." Aunt Holly looked out at the trees again. "We're just more alike than she'd care to admit."

My mother adjusted the front of her dress and turned abruptly to go inside.

"How CAN YOU do this to me?" My grandmother stood in the middle of the kitchen, still holding the plates. Two chickens perched on the back of the kitchen chairs. My grandfather was squeezing a dropper into their eyes.

"How could you even think about bringing them into the house?"

"I put paper on the floor." Grampa Cole pointed to the *New York Times* neatly folded below their tail feathers. A few droppings had already fallen. "I had to bring them in. They both have eye infections, so I have to keep putting these drops in. Their metabolism is so fast, they need twice the dosage."

Aunt Holly and Joanne stood in the doorway. Joanne still clutched her marshmallow stick.

He looked at my grandmother when she didn't say anything. "June, if you could only learn to like them—"

"How would you feel if I told you I was having an affair?"

"What?" gasped my mother.

"I just want to know how he'd feel," said Gramma June, sounding suddenly embarrassed. "If it would matter."

"Of course it would matter," said my mother.

Gramma June looked back at my grandfather. She shook her head. "Oh, I don't think so, Marion. Because he's just shut me out. I'm so tired of his mind always being elsewhere—"

"*Stop* it!" yelled Grampa Cole. "Both of you." He rarely raised his voice. It was enough to silence all of us.

His anger subsided into great gentleness as he

carefully picked up the chickens and cradled one in each elbow. His eyes had grown glassy. I'd never seen him come that close to tears. I didn't think Gramma June had either, as she touched his arm, whispering, "Oh, I'm sorry." He could only nod, brushing past us to his den.

My mother was the first to move. She took the dishes from my grandmother and piled them into the sink as quietly as if someone were sleeping. Gramma June collapsed into a chair. She stared at the bowl of apples in the middle of the table.

"Maybe he can't help it," I said.

"Maybe he can't help forgetting," added Joanne.

I resisted reaching out to hold her hand the way we used to on walks at Indian Lake looking for salamanders.

My grandmother slowly revolved the bowl, examining it from every angle. "Do you know that in forty-one years of marriage I've never known what he's really thinking? I could never even guess. Once I came right out and asked him—only once. He told me he wasn't thinking at all. He was singing a church hymn to himself." She smiled sadly at Joanne and me. "Maybe."

My mother sat down opposite Gramma June. "Do you really think about that? About having an ... affair?"

Gramma June picked out an apple, dangling it by its stem. "That doesn't mean I actually would."

Aunt Holly leaned over to hug Gramma June. "Thoughts can't hurt you."

Gramma June relaxed against Aunt Holly and closed her eyes. She reached up to hold onto Aunt Holly's arms.

My mother looked away from them, at her own hands resting on the edge of the table. She stretched her fingers apart and pressed them into the wood. They suddenly seemed unnaturally long and cumbersome to me. As if they did to her as well, she withdrew her hands and sat on them. I knew her then as that little girl who quietly played with her china dolls. I saw her at my age, twirling that confirmation cross around her neck, cherishing it like a good-luck charm. I saw her sitting on her bed and sitting on her hands. She would have stared at her lap as she did now, listening to voices just outside her room or downstairs. Listening for someone to knock on her door and ask if anything was wrong.

She stood up, saying, "Well, we can't leave those dishes sitting there all night, can we?"

"No, and I suppose it's my turn anyway," said Gramma June, getting up slowly.

"I don't mind. I really don't mind." She turned her back to Gramma June and Aunt Holly as she filled the sink. "You two can dry."

I WENT OUTSIDE to find Jack. He'd fallen asleep in the hammock and I stood so that my shadow in the porch light fell across his face. He opened his eyes.

"Can I lie with you?"

"Sure."

He made room for me. I was glad it was dark enough so that I couldn't quite see his face. I leaned over and kissed him on the lips.

For me, it was the first romantic moment of my life. I felt both exhilarated and terrified. But as I drew away he laughed. "What was that for?" he asked, in a tone of voice like my father's when I'd crawl into his lap to give him a big hug.

I shrugged. "Nothing." I looked up, trying to lose myself in the pattern of leaves against the bluish-black sky. But I started thinking about my grandfather. I'd never thought that he'd sing hymns to himself, if only because he always seemed so restless during church. Just as I'd never thought that my grandparents might not be as close as I'd always imagined.

MY GRANDFATHER HAD fallen asleep on the couch in his den. Gramma June spread a blanket over him. She placed fresh newspapers under the chickens, where they now perched on his desk chair. I watched her from the doorway and saw how she peered at their infected eyes, at the lids half shut like filmy blue shades. Then for a moment she sat on the edge of the couch. She rested her hand on Grampa Cole's chest, as if to feel how it rose and fell.

———

I WOKE IN the middle of the night to the sound of the back door. I knew it was my mother before I even looked out the window. She walked into the pen and opened the coop.

"I just wanted to look at them," she said when I joined her. She reached in to touch one of the chickens. "Oh, they're so soft. I never knew they'd be so soft. As if they have no skeleton. No bones."

"That's why they don't catch cold," I said, with some authority. "Because they have so many feathers."

She stared into the coop as I remembered her staring into our living room when it was being repainted, the furniture hidden beneath white cloths. "The room might as well be empty," she had said longingly. "We might as well not have lived here at all."

In the porch light I could see those lines of worry coursing like rivers. "It will be good to see your father, don't you think?" she asked.

Her voice was tiny. I was angry at how easily it rose up and became lost like the seeds we liked to blow from dandelions. She used to tell me we were blowing the seeds back to God so that He could replant them.

I wanted her to look at me. I scraped my finger against a wire tip in the mesh, scraping until I cut through the skin. I was glad when I began to bleed.

I held up my finger. "Mom."

"Oh, Leslie," she exclaimed, jumping up. She rushed

over to me and held my hand so she could see it in the light. "Is it deep?"

"Not really."

"We'd better go inside and clean it out right away."

MY MOTHER WAS rinsing my finger at the kitchen sink when Gramma June came in. "What's the matter? What's going on? I thought I heard someone," she said, tying her bathrobe belt. She wore the slippers with the roses my mother had embroidered into the toes one Christmas.

"Leslie cut herself," said my mother, without looking up.

"She cut herself? Oh, how did she do that? Let me see."

"She's fine."

"But you better put something on it, an antiseptic, I'll go get some . . ." Gramma June was already heading for her medicine cabinet when my mother whipped around and said, "I can take care of her myself."

Gramma June stopped in the doorway. "Oh. Well then." She looked down at her slippers. "I guess I'll just go back to bed then. I guess I'll just leave you two alone." She left, shuffling down the hall.

"Oh, dear," my mother sighed, drying her hands on a dish towel and leaving it rumpled on the rack.

But I was pleased with her for standing up to my

grandmother, if only because I'd never seen her do that before. "You *can* take care of me yourself," I said.

"I suppose," she said distractedly, cupping my chin and examining my face as she would in searching for my father's features.

CHAPTER

THREE

My mother had always played with me after school. We'd pretend that the living room rug was the ocean and the couch our cruise ship, or we'd build mansions across the floor by propping up books as walls. Our house had felt like a haven then, a secret place, with only my mother's birds to watch us, the glass blue jays on the mantelpiece, the wooden parrot hanging above the couch, the planter in the shape of a swan filled with geraniums. A row of sea gulls perched on the piano as I'd seen real ones perch at the beach in Connecticut. Then there were those birds so small only my mother and I really knew they were there, like the woodpeckers clustered on top of the thermostat.

At the beginning of sixth grade, I started to lose interest in those games, preferring to change the clothes on a doll or two alone in my room. And sometimes I'd pray. My mother had passed on to me her cross necklace at my own confirmation, and I liked to think that I was now capable of her same closeness with God, with that greater something outside of myself. But usually I'd end up writing poems about frosty moons in a special ring-bound notebook.

One afternoon she was sitting with me at the kitchen table while I ate my snack. I told her about the essay I wrote during English and who won the card games of Spit at lunch. I twisted my fingers around the sugar spoon handle to illustrate the routine I was learning on the uneven bars. I unfolded my day for her like a story as I did every afternoon. Her eyes were always bright, her lips slightly parted.

When I was finished, she said, "Bridget and Celia are waiting for you."

Bridget and Celia were my two oldest dolls.

"It's Celia's birthday—I bet you'd forgotten that," said my mother. "They're about to have a party and they didn't want to start without you."

I tried to see myself in the spoon. "I didn't forget."

I followed her into the living room. Bridget and Celia, along with my other dolls and my stuffed animals, were arranged around Kleenex boxes turned upside down as tables. The miniature pin-the-tail-on-the-donkey my mother had made out of felt was pinned to the footrest of the armchair. Celebrating my dolls' birthdays was my favorite of all the games my mother and I played after school. It was my mother's favorite game too. But now the sight of my dolls' faces frozen into their usual expressions bored me.

"Mommy, I don't think I really feel like playing today."

She was already kneeling on the floor by one of the tables. "No?"

"Not really."

She set upright a plastic cup the size of a thimble, in front of my giraffe. "I just had it in mind that it was Celia's birthday."

"Sorry."

She stood up and kissed my forehead. "That's all right." She laughed, brushing lint from the wool rug off her skirt. "I certainly have enough to do. All that awful ironing I keep putting off until your father doesn't have a single shirt left."

I helped her collect the cups into one of the Kleenex boxes.

"Thanks, honey."

After that, my mother no longer pulled out my dolls. She smiled good-naturedly at me when I got up from my snacks. Once I looked back at her where she still sat at the table. She wasn't facing me but I saw her reflection in the toaster. Her smile had already faded.

I CAME HOME one afternoon to find a plate of brownies covered with aluminum foil on the kitchen table. I was surprised to hear my mother talking to someone in the living room, since she rarely ever had anybody over, and never after school. I peeled off the foil and carried the plate into the living room.

My mother sat on the couch beside a woman I'd never seen before. The woman seemed too big for the room; her knees were pressed against the coffee table and the teacup nestled in her palm seemed as small as one of my dolls'. My mother had arranged her tea set on the good silver tray that had grapes and flowers engraved around its edges.

"Leslie, you're home," said my mother, as if she hadn't been expecting me. "I'd like you to meet Mrs. Bowman."

Mrs. Bowman smiled at me. She wore braces, something I'd never seen on an adult before. I pressed my finger into the crumbs around my brownies.

"Mrs. Bowman is here to help me pick out material for the new slipcovers," said my mother, patting the couch. "For the chair too."

Mrs. Bowman smiled again. For a moment I had thought she might be someone special; my mother usually had over people like Mrs. Bowman only when I was in school.

"You know what, honey? Mrs. Bowman's husband cuts Daddy's hair. At that barbershop next to the deli where you used to buy your animal crackers."

My mother crossed her legs, pointing one slender white shoe. She wore one of her best skirts, one that seemed to cascade around her, filling the couch and skimming the floor. It was the pink of almost-ripe strawberries, the same shade as her lipstick. She suddenly seemed beautiful to me, but I was more used to feeling my mother than seeing her, feeling the way she could whip up around me like a cool breeze. I sat in the armchair, balancing the plate of brownies on my lap.

"He's been getting his hair cut there ever since we moved here, when he first got a position at the college. Leslie was two when we moved. Has Sam been working there that long?"

Mrs. Bowman took one of the brownies from a plate on the tray. "Oh, longer than that."

"Well, Dale has never wanted to go to anyone else." My mother poured a drop of tea into Mrs. Bowman's already full cup. "This town has become so built up since then, hasn't it? I remember when you could drive down Blackberry Road and it was all trees. Nothing but trees. Leslie even remembers that."

"No, I don't."

"Well, you do. I used to stop so we could see the ducks on that pond there." She looked back at Mrs. Bowman. "I grew up in Connecticut and have always missed those woods, and we were right near the beach as well. It's only three hours away but you'd never know it."

"We have some relatives in Connecticut."

"*Have* you?" my mother exclaimed.

Mrs. Bowman nodded vaguely. She was looking around at my mother's birds and I looked around at them too. They seemed surprisingly lifeless.

"It's beautiful, isn't it? My parents still live there so we spend most of our summers with them. Leslie and I anyway. Dale comes out on weekends. Leslie loves it out there, don't you?"

Before I could answer my mother continued. "There's a wonderful inlet that's perfect for small children because it's so shallow. We used to spend whole afternoons wading and catching hermit crabs. They're so tiny," said my mother, squinting at her fingers as she pinched them together, "and they have the funniest little faces."

Mrs. Bowman looked at my mother curiously.

"That, of course, was when she was small," said my mother, recrossing her legs. She examined the hem of her skirt.

Mrs. Bowman tucked her napkin beside her saucer.

57

"Dale grew up there too. We went to high school together."

"Ah, high school sweethearts," said Mrs. Bowman, checking her watch. "I have another appointment tonight so I suppose we should get going on this."

"Yes, I guess so," said my mother quietly.

I was glad Mrs. Bowman interrupted my mother before she could go on about my father as she sometimes would to me when he'd retreat to his study right after dinner. How he could have inherited his father's lumberyard business if he hadn't grown restless and wanted to leave. She'd followed him to college, then graduate school, living in tiny studio apartments with only a hot plate for a stove. They had to wash their dishes in the bathroom sink. My mother had to work overtime at the A&P or behind a deli counter. Then they had moved to New Jersey, into our ranch-style white-shingled home just like all the other ranch-style white-shingled houses on our street. My mother had painted the front door lavender and hung elaborate flower boxes in all the windows, trying to make our house special.

"Are you planning to redecorate the entire room?" Mrs. Bowman asked.

"All I know is I'm tired of this," said my mother, dismissing the rust-colored room with a wave of her hand.

Mrs. Bowman frowned, opening one of the large books of material stacked between them.

My mother traced her finger through the pattern of autumn leaves on the old slipcovers. "You must see a lot of houses. They must all look alike after a while."

"Oh, I don't know about that," said Mrs. Bowman. "I don't know anyone who has as many birds as you do."

My mother picked up a ceramic peacock from the coffee table. "This is my favorite." She held it out to Mrs. Bowman, who made no move to touch it. Replacing the peacock, she briefly stroked its glazed feathers. "Do you have children?"

"Four."

"You're lucky. I would have had more, but I had three miscarriages before Leslie, and I only had her because they made me lie in bed. I wasn't allowed up at all except to go to the bathroom. Imagine that." She looked at me longingly. "Leslie's my miracle."

Mrs. Bowman shifted so that her knees knocked against the table, setting the china to rattle softly. For something to do, I reached for my mother's cup.

"You don't like tea," said my mother.

"Yes, I do." I pulled my legs up onto the chair so that I could cradle the cup between my knees. I didn't care that my underwear showed.

Mrs. Bowman laughed. It was a laugh that sprang up from deep inside her, like a coil. "You never know when they'll start liking things," she said. "Next it will be fish."

I swallowed a large mouthful of the bitter brown liquid. Mrs. Bowman winked at me.

"Why are you wearing braces?" I asked.

"That's not polite, Leslie," my mother snapped.

"It's all right," said Mrs. Bowman. "My kids think it's pretty funny too." She leaned toward me and whispered as if telling me a secret, "Because I should have worn them at *your* age."

"I know she doesn't like tea," said my mother.

"Why don't we do this," said Mrs. Bowman wearily. "You pick out five or six swatches that appeal to you. From that maybe you'll be able to get some idea of what you would like to do with the room."

My mother pulled one of her needlepoint pillows into her lap. "Fine."

I had long since finished my brownies. The room had grown shadowy in a way I didn't remember it ever being when my mother and I played in here together. I carefully replaced the cup on my mother's saucer and stood up.

Mrs. Bowman reached out her hand. "Nice meeting you, Leslie."

I wasn't used to people shaking my hand. Hers was large and coarse, unlike my mother's which was always soft and warm. "Yeah."

My mother didn't say anything to me. She pulled another pillow into her lap. As I was going upstairs

I heard her say to Mrs. Bowman, "She writes poetry now."

AFTER SCHOOL A few days later, my mother said, "I think I've narrowed it down to three swatches." She wore one of my father's old shirts, one with a tomato juice stain down the front. Her face seemed transparent without makeup and I knew she hadn't been out of the house all day.

She crossed her arms on the kitchen table. "I'd like your opinion."

Decorating didn't interest me, but my mother had never asked for my "opinion" before. "Sure," I said, shrugging.

On the back of the couch she had draped the three swatches. One was pastel pink roses against a deeper pink. The other two were a thinly striped blue and yellow and a plain lavender.

"I just don't know," said my mother. "Which do you like?"

The roses seemed most like my mother because I was used to her wearing pink. I actually liked that one best but for some reason I chose the striped.

My mother rubbed her thumb across the swatch. "I guess I kind of like this too. But it will be hard to match with the walls, don't you think? The only color I can think of is white—anything else, this would kill."

"Make them white, then," I said, yawning.

She chewed her lower lip. "I could. But you know, I had blue in mind. Light blue walls."

"The pink would go with blue walls."

She nodded. "I do like the roses. Pink and blue could be too much, though."

I lay on the couch and flapped my dress to fan air onto my legs.

"That's not particularly ladylike," said my mother.

"It's hot in here."

"What about just plain?" she asked. "Too dull?"

"I told you what I like. I like the stripes."

"I'll tell you what." She sat next to me. "Let's narrow it down to two and then let Daddy make the final choice." She took the swatches and ironed them out with the edge of her hand on the coffee table. "Now, besides the stripes, which other do you like best?"

"The plain one, I like the plain one."

"*Do* you?"

"Yes, I do. I really, really do."

She swept the swatches together. "Go and do whatever it is you want."

I sat a moment longer.

"Go *on*," she said.

"I don't know why you don't believe me," I said.

"Because I know you," she said. "You like the pink, like me. You like the roses."

I flipped open the tail of the duck cigarette holder. We used to pretend it was a boat and sail it across the rug.

She gently pinched the back of my neck. "Go on. We'll see what Daddy has to say."

UPSTAIRS IN MY room I undressed one of my dolls, taking off a dress my mother had crocheted and replacing it with a store-bought one that had a zipper. When I had a poem shaped in my head, I stretched out on the floor and wrote it down in my notebook, carefully curling the tails of g's and y's. I lay like that until my father came home.

At dinner my mother told him how she had spent the day picking out material for the slipcovers. She had put on makeup and changed into a dress laced with pink.

"Anyway, I think we've narrowed it down to two choices," she said. "With Leslie's help, that is."

"Has our little girl inherited her mother's fine taste?" He winked at my mother.

She hid a pleased smile, combing the fringe on her place mat. "We want you to make the final decision." She drew out the swatches from her dress pocket and unrolled them in front of him.

He laughed, rubbing his face. "I don't know how clearheaded I am right now to make such an important decision."

"It won't be hard," said my mother. "You always know exactly what you like."

I had expected her to include the roses. The swatches from her pocket were the stripes and the plain one. He pointed to the plain.

My mother crinkled her nose. "Really?"

"Honey, you asked me what I liked. If you want me to tell you I like the stripes, then I like the stripes."

"Maybe you should look at them in the living room. It's hard, after all, to tell from such a small piece what the overall effect will be. It just might be too much lavender."

"Honestly, Marion, I'm not good at these things." He looked at me. "What does Leslie think, anyway?"

My mother flicked her fork against her water glass. "*She* doesn't care either."

"I do so," I said weakly.

"I don't know why you two can't show a little more interest," she said. "You have to live with it too."

"I've never disliked anything you've chosen before," said my father patiently.

"You just like anything you're used to. Those slip-covers could be worn through and you'd still like them."

My father buttered his roll with long strokes of his knife.

"You know, I would rather not have to redecorate

at all," said my mother, "because whenever it comes time to fix up this place, I think how we've been stuck in this godforsaken town how many years longer—"

"I'm *tired*, Marion," said my father. "And you know, don't you, that if I'd picked the other one in the first place, you'd want me to pick the plain."

My mother looked down at her plate.

He reached across the table to caress her hand. "Isn't that true?"

She withdrew her hands into her lap. "I *hate* living here."

My father leaned back and drummed his fingers on the edge of the table. "And where would you like to go? Where do you think you would be happier?"

"Anywhere. I need a change."

"We don't need to move for you to get a change. Maybe you should try doing some volunteer work. Get a part-time job—"

"I want to move back to Connecticut."

He rubbed his face. "We can't move back to Connecticut."

"Why not?"

"Marion, be realistic. I have a good, steady position at the college here. I can't just give that up."

"You can if you really want to."

He leaned forward. "I don't want to. I don't want to return to our roots. And honestly, sweetheart, I don't think you'd be happier there. I don't think you'd be happier *anywhere*."

"How can you say that? That's a terrible thing to say."

"I just meant that . . ." He sighed. "I'm sorry."

But she was already getting up. In the next moment she'd left through the front door.

My insides constricted as they would whenever she got upset and left like that, heading aimlessly down the street. And my father would always go out after her as he did now.

"Finish your dinner," he said. "You've hardly eaten a thing."

I picked at my lima beans until they returned. He had his arm around her as he led her back to the table and pulled out her chair. She seemed more cheerful, telling me that if I didn't finish my meat I'd be lacking in protein and unable to spin around those uneven bars.

When we were finished, my father folded his napkin and got up.

"Where are you going?" she asked.

"I have an exam to write up for tomorrow."

She only nodded. Then she asked, "Dale? Do I bore you?"

"What?" he laughed.

"I was just wondering. If you've perhaps grown a little . . . tired of me."

"I have an *exam* to write up, Marion."

"I know," she said gently. "I understand. But . . . besides that."

He laughed again, unfolding his napkin to refold it. "You're too much. Too much," he only said. He squeezed my shoulder as he left the room.

We heard him climb the stairs, then the squeak of his study chair. When I was younger, he'd let me play at his typewriter while he worked at his desk. I'd bang on the keys, half hoping he'd ask me to quiet down, but he hardly ever moved except to lean back in his chair.

I expected my mother to go on about my father. She didn't. She'd grown as still as when she prayed in church. But I knew she wasn't praying because when she lifted her head and drew herself up as if taking a deep breath there was not that look of calm I was used to. She stared blankly out the window.

"Mom?"

She began to pile the dishes.

I gathered up the glasses.

"I don't need your help," she said.

"I don't mind."

She frowned at me and I suddenly felt embarrassed.

"Go do your homework," she said, pushing open the swinging kitchen door with her back. "Go disappear like your father."

I sat at my desk and listened to my mother doing the dishes. Plates clinked noisily together. I thought about how my father had laughed and played with his napkin. How he hadn't been able to answer her.

Finally there was the sound of the dishwasher. I wondered what room my mother had gone into. The back door slammed. I looked out my window and saw her run across the lawn stamping her feet and clapping her hands at our neighbor's cat. She ran out of her shoes.

The cat leapt into the bushes with something gray hanging from his mouth. My mother crouched in front of the bushes but must have lost sight of the cat because she walked slowly back toward the house. She stopped in front of the full birdbath and lifted out a leaf. I thought she would toss it into the grass. Instead, she placed it back on the water and gave it a push. When it slowed down, she pushed it again. And again. I was able to see her now as I had seen her with Mrs. Bowman on the couch. But this time she wasn't beautiful—she was far away. I threw open the window.

She looked up at me, her finger poised over the leaf. "Did he get a bird?"

She wiped her hand on her dress. "I couldn't see."

"Is it still warm out?"

She nodded. "It's nice."

"Do you want to play Frisbee?"

"You've finished your homework already?"

"Yes," I lied.

She picked up her shoes and clicked their heels together. "If you've finished your homework."

68

We threw the Frisbee around until dark, my mother's dress billowing as she ran across the grass. Neither of us was very good at catching it but it was a game my mother never tired of. She burst out laughing when she just missed the Frisbee and fell so that her dress wound up around her thighs. If she'd fallen like that in front of anyone else, even my father, she wouldn't have been able to laugh like that. But it was only me. And as I watched the Frisbee sail through the air, watched without feeling like chasing after it, I wished there was someone else there. I wished my father would have been watching from his study window. But even before I looked up I knew he wouldn't be; he'd already be lost in his work.

MY MOTHER SETTLED on a dark-blue floral pattern for the slipcovers, having left it up to Mrs. Bowman herself to decide.

FOUR

Over the next year, I came to dread coming home, unable to escape to my room without feeling that somehow I had abandoned my mother, having to listen to her clean out desk drawers and wax the tabletops, things she never used to have to do in the afternoons.

Now that I was in junior high, if I didn't have gymnastics practice or other activities at school, I was with my friends at the mall, buying imitation-silk blouses that my mother pleaded with me not to wear because they made me look "cheap."

I'D BEGUN REALLY to miss having brothers and sisters and was particularly happy to be at Indian Lake the summer of seventh grade. Joanne had been wanting to show me something ever since we arrived. One afternoon she asked me to paddle out with her in the canoe, and as we turned a bend into a cove she pointed through the trees. "There."

I could just see the barn-red siding of a house. We pulled the canoe far up onto shore so that it was hidden. I followed her through the trees along what seemed to be her own path to the house.

Beneath the windows of the screened porch the paint was peeling off in thick sheets. The lawn was completely overgrown, the tall grasses bending in the lake breezes so that they shone like silver. The house was small and squat, and seemed to crouch there like our neighbor's cat eyeing the birds in my mother's garden back home.

"You know who lives here?" I asked.

"Does it really *look* to you like anyone's living here?" asked Joanne. "No one's been here all summer. It reminds me of this old lady on our block who died—no one wanted to deal with cleaning out her things, so they just let her house sit there for months."

Joanne ran across the lawn to a fir tree that hugged one corner of the house. Reaching under it, she pulled out what I recognized as one of the old spaghetti pots we used to keep our salamanders in. She overturned the pot beneath one of the porch windows and, stepping on it, pushed herself through the screen where she'd pulled back a flap.

"You're crazy!" I called, trying to whisper.

"Just come on."

I thought about waiting for her in the canoe. But I didn't like standing there by myself listening to the rustling and creaking of the birches. I ran through the long grasses to the house, their blades scraping at my knees as if they were trying to hold me back.

"I can't believe you cut this hole," I said, struggling through the screen. It had looked much easier for Joanne.

"I didn't. It was already torn, I just tore it a little more."

There wasn't much to look at on the porch, a couple of fold-up beach chairs, a lopsided TV stand, a fish tank green with algae and empty except for an overturned plastic castle. There was a small bureau missing its knobs and bottom drawer. A few battered hardcover books stood on top of the bureau, between a pair of leprechaun bookends. The leprechauns leaned back against the books with their legs sprawled and their green hats drooped to one side. Above the windows hung a shelf stretching the entire length of the porch. It was lined with fish skulls.

She saw me looking at the skulls and climbed onto the chest to take one down. "Aren't they cool?" she asked, digging a finger into an eye socket.

"Who would go around saving fish skulls?" I asked.

"He was probably just proud of the fish he caught."

"He?"

"I think it was a he. Besides, look at these." She pulled open the top chest drawer. In among a pair of garden clippers, a miniature magnetic backgammon set, packs of cards and flashlights was a ceramic pencil holder filled with pipes. "He loved the lake," said Joanne, rearranging the pipes as if they were flowers in a vase. "He probably lived here all his life."

"You think he's dead then?"

"Look in here. It's just the way he left it."

I cupped my hands around my face so that I could see through one of the windows to the kitchen. There was a blue cup on a table directly below the window. The bottom of the cup was brown with what looked like old coffee.

"He probably died right after breakfast one morning," said Joanne.

"You're giving me the creeps."

"I like that. To think his spirit could be here right now, floating around us. You believe in spirits, don't you? I mean, you believe in God."

"I never said I believed in God."

"Well, your mother does. I thought she brought you up that way."

"She did. That doesn't mean *I* have to believe." I'd stopped wearing the cross, having decided that praying was foolish, that I might as well be talking to myself.

Joanne sat in one of the fold-up chairs and crossed

her arms. She smiled as proudly as if she owned the place. "So what do you think?"

"Don't you know this is breaking and entering?"

She frowned. "It's not like I'm actually going into the house."

I kept expecting to hear a car in the driveway or for someone to burst through the door leading from the porch into the kitchen. I stayed close to the hole in the screen. "Why do you come here?"

"To be alone, I guess."

"You can go for a walk in the woods to be alone."

"Yeah, but . . . I don't know. Anyway, you have to swear not to tell anyone about this place. If Jack found out, forget it. He'd come in here and party, tear the place apart. And sweet, sweet Meg. She'd for sure tell Mom. Mom who thinks she's an angel."

"I thought you and Meg got along."

"Meg? She's an airhead. All she thinks about is boys. Boys, boys, boys. It's really gross. She's forever falling in love."

Perhaps Meg did think mostly about boys. But I couldn't help admiring how easily she was able to attract them. Boys from around the lake seemed to drop by regularly to see her. Her most recent boyfriend, Chris, would run his hands through her hair as they sat together at the end of the dock. Her hair had grown out so that it now fell in soft curls around her ears. He'd massage her neck. I knew Meg was secretly thrilled; she spent long sessions in front of her mirror layering on waterproof mascara and eye shadow before he would come by for only a swim. But she was able to act as if she didn't care, lightly kicking up the water and watching it drip off her toes.

"Seems like guys are always falling in love with her too," I said.

"If you want to call it that."

"What do you mean?"

"I don't know . . ." Joanne took down one of the books and peered at a page, running her finger along a line. "I just wouldn't call it love exactly." She held up the cover. "I'm reading *Moby Dick* now."

"Then what do you call it?"

"I don't *know*." She leafed quickly through the pages. "This is really quite brilliant."

I was annoyed with her for changing the subject. "Brilliant?" I laughed. "How do *you* know it's brilliant?"

She slammed the book shut. "Because I've been reading all summer. I've probably read more books this summer than you have in your whole life."

Joanne suddenly seemed frail to me, her arms and legs protruding bonily from her oversized T-shirt and baggy army-green shorts. Her feet looked large in her Pro-Ked sneakers. But I knew that, like Meg, she could probably have any boy she wanted; at Christmas we'd stood by the tree gently spinning the gold balls, and she'd confided that she'd already French-kissed, something I hadn't yet experienced. I'd envied how well put together she had looked, in a low-cut red sweater, black miniskirt and short leather boots. As for me, nothing ever fit right. Sweaters hung on my thin shoulders as limply as they did on the hanger and skirts sagged at my waist.

The porch seemed to be closing in on us, the shadows growing deeper in the corners as the sun moved to the other side of the house. I focused on the castle in the fish tank, trying to shake the feeling that someone was actually there listening to us. The castle had fallen on a scuba diver. I could just see his head and one tank the size of a battery. "We should get back," I said.

"We just got here."

"I want to go back."

Joanne now hugged the book, losing it in the folds of her T-shirt. "Great."

JOANNE NEVER AGAIN asked me to come along with her. I felt that I had disappointed her, that as much as she liked being alone she would have enjoyed sharing her secret place with me. But I couldn't understand how she could prefer sitting on someone else's porch, reading someone else's dusty old classics, to her family.

———

ONE MORNING I was sunbathing with Meg and Aunt Holly down at the beach. We lay on our stomachs with our bikini tops untied. Joanne was pushing the canoe into the water.

"What do you do out in the canoe all that time anyway?" asked Meg without opening her eyes.

"None of your business."

"I just asked a question."

"I'm looking for muskrats, all right?"

Aunt Holly propped herself up on one elbow, holding her top in place. "Good luck, sweetie."

"Thanks, Mom," said Joanne, her head down as she buckled her life preserver.

Aunt Holly watched her paddle out of sight around the peninsula.

"What it really is," said Meg, "is that she wants a boyfriend. And she could have one, she's pretty enough. But no boy wants a mopey girl like that."

"Oh, she'll grow out of it. Give her a little time," said Aunt Holly, resettling herself on her stomach. "Besides, you've had *your* mopey moments too."

Meg's mouth fell open in mock surprise. "I have not."

"At least when Joanne mopes she disappears to do it. You hang around for all of us to see your pouts that hang down to your knees."

"I do *not* pout."

"Oh yeah?" Aunt Holly pulled on Meg's top so that it slipped down.

"Mom!" Meg squealed, gently slapping her mother's hands away.

I liked how Meg and Aunt Holly were able to tease each other, and they shared in a way that I thought only best friends could share; one night after dinner I'd overheard Meg asking Aunt Holly about waxing her legs. She was leaning against the bathroom doorjamb watching Aunt Holly rinse out a sink full of underwear. She told Aunt Holly that Chris didn't like that "stubbly feel" from shaving. They spent the rest of the evening in the bathroom, Aunt Holly running back and forth from the stove with cubes of wax she was melting in a saucepan. I couldn't imagine ever being able to talk that openly with my own mother.

"Leslie."

I looked up. My mother crouched beside me. "Please. Put your top on."

"It is on. It's just not tied."

"Well, I wish you would tie it."

"No one can see, Mom. We're on our stomachs."

"Why don't you join us?" Aunt Holly asked.

My mother hugged herself as she did that summer whenever my aunt suggested she join us; I knew she resented the time I spent with Aunt Holly. But Aunt Holly knew how to enjoy herself in a way that my mother just didn't, at least not outside of the games we used to play. If I wasn't sunbathing, I was polishing my nails as Aunt Holly, Meg and I sat with our fingers spread across the picnic table, or else I was lounging on the porch where we shared a pitcher of grape Kool-Aid, Aunt Holly's favorite.

My mother looked back at me. "Please," she whispered.

I reached around and tied it.

"Thank you, sweetheart."

She stumbled back up the sandy embankment, reaching for branches as if she were climbing a steep cliff. She'd spent most of the afternoon by herself, lying in the hammock that hung between two birch trees out on the peninsula. At night, when the rest of us played cards, she'd retreat into a corner to sort through her huge bag of scrap material for the quilt she planned to make. She'd arrange and rearrange the scraps across the couch and sometimes the floor, trying to decide on a pattern.

My mother lay back down in the hammock and for a long moment stared at us. Finally she turned her head away to gaze out at the lake. As I untied my suit again, Aunt Holly winked at me.

ONE AFTERNOON, WE were all finishing lunch down by the lake when Aunt Holly happened to mention that they were considering buying a camper.

"A camper?" said my mother. "What are you going to do with a camper?"

"What anyone does," said Aunt Holly. "Travel. Or just keep it around as extra room. Instead of adding onto the house like we were thinking about."

"The kids will be going to college soon, won't they? It doesn't seem like you would need extra room."

"Well, that doesn't necessarily mean they won't be here during the summers anymore."

My mother peeled an apple so that the skin was falling away in a single coil. "Seems rather extravagant to me."

"Of course it does."

"Of course?"

"You've always hyped about how we spend our money," said Aunt Holly, sounding bored. "You know that."

"It's none of my business how you spend your money."

"No, as a matter of fact, it's not."

"But I'm your sister."

"Marion . . ." began my father.

"I can't help it. Why haven't I ever been able to say a word around her?"

Aunt Holly laughed. "Why *haven't* you?"

"You've never listened to me."

"Marion, don't do this," said my father.

My mother looked back at her apple. The coil broke and fell into the sand. She continued to scrape at the apple, flinging the last of the skin off like wood carvings. "She's just always been right about everything! Why has she always been right about everything?"

"What?" Aunt Holly laughed again, more loudly this time.

"With all the grief you've always caused our parents. With all that worrying, even *they* now think you can do no wrong. But who's always been there for them, who stayed up all night with Mother, listening to her cry, when you just disappeared, leaving just a note saying you'd call when you'd reached New Orleans?"

"Marion," said Aunt Holly, as quietly as if coaxing a child. "Where's this coming from?"

My mother wouldn't look up from her apple. "It's just that now it's my daughter you're taking away from me."

My face instantly became flushed. Joanne was staring at me. "Mom . . ." I didn't know what else to say.

"You're turning her against me."

Aunt Holly looked at me, frowning. "Am I turning you against your mother?"

"No . . ."

"No, I didn't think I was. You're just sounding as jealous as you always have, Marion. Always jealous over nothing. You sound exactly like you did back when you were ten and always accusing me of taking your toys."

"You did take my toys! You were always taking everything of mine!"

"Marion," my father snapped. "If you could only *hear* yourself."

My mother placed the apple on her plate and the peeler beside the apple. "See?" she said, looking at my aunt. "You're just stealing away everyone I love!" She left us, running up the driveway to the road.

My father scanned the lake as he sometimes did to see if any fish were jumping. Over the past year my mother had begun to worry so over him. She worried that he no longer cared about spending time with her— he'd begun writing for various periodicals, in addition to teaching extra classes, so he spent more and more time in his study. She worried that he no longer really loved her.

I watched him, waiting. And I saw that everyone else was watching him too.

"I'm sorry, guys," he finally said, raising his hands in surrender. "I'm really sorry."

As he walked down to the dock, I realized he wasn't so much apologizing for my mother as for the fact that, for the first time, he could not bring himself to go after her. He grabbed his fishing pole and got into the old green boat. In a moment he had motored out of sight.

———

UNCLE RYAN WAS starting a fire in the grill and Joanne and I were outside husking corn for dinner when my mother finally returned. I'd begun to worry, but now that I knew she was safe I didn't want to look at her. I didn't want to see the pine needles dangling from her hair and blouse, the mud drying around the edges of her sandals. She must have walked miles.

"I left the salad for you," said Aunt Holly through the screen door.

"I'd like to put these in water if that's okay," said my mother, holding up a spindly bouquet of Queen Anne's lace.

"There are plenty of jelly jars in the kitchen," called Aunt Holly, already leaving the door.

"And what do you have there?" asked Uncle Ryan, patting one of my mother's bulging skirt pockets.

Shyly she pulled out a handful of pinecones. They weren't much larger than jellybeans.

He laughed softly. "What did you do, raid the entire forest?"

"Is Dale around?"

"He went to the store to get some beer," I said, picking the last threads of silk from an ear of corn.

"Oh. Well, I guess I'll just go freshen up then."

When we'd finished the corn, I followed her into our room. She was taking out the pinecones from her pockets and laying them, one by one, on the bureau.

When she saw me, she said, "Aren't these the smallest cones you've ever seen?"

"Why did you have to go and act like that? Why do you have to be so paranoid? Aunt Holly's not doing anything. No one's taking me away from anybody . . ." I felt as if I was about to cry, but I refused to cry in front of her.

"I'm sorry I embarrassed you."

"*Yes*, you embarrassed me. And you embarrassed Daddy."

At the mention of my father she fumbled and dropped a couple of cones onto the floor.

I sat on their bed. "I just wish you and Aunt Holly could get along better."

"You wish I was different."

"I didn't say that."

She sat down heavily beside me. "You know you do."

Lately I liked to think that my mother didn't know me at all. But now she made me feel as exposed as if she'd caught me watching myself in the mirror and turning my head this way and that. I did wish she was different. And I wished that I wasn't so afraid of becoming just like her. These facts now lay between us as plainly as the cards she used to spread out into a pond so that we could play Go Fish. So plainly I couldn't deny them. Nor did she seem to expect me to deny them, as she took off her dusty sandals and dropped them onto the floor. With her fingers she combed the pine needles from her hair. "Well, maybe I wish I were different too," she said.

I FORCED MYSELF to stay awake that night, wondering if my parents would talk in bed like they sometimes did. If my father would ask where she'd been all afternoon. He didn't. She'd placed the jar of Queen Anne's lace beside their bed. As he sat on the edge of the bed, he stared blankly at the flowers as if he weren't quite seeing them. "Marion, you can't go around doing and saying whatever you please like that," he said. "It's not right."

She'd curled herself against his back. "I'm sorry."

He pried away her arms. "Let's go to sleep."

"Will you hold me?"

"I'll hold you." He turned out the light.

"Dale?"

I heard how he caressed her, maybe her shoulder, his hand moving back and forth along her nightgown.

"I'm so . . . lonely."

He stopped caressing her and for a moment the night held itself still like a drop of water about to fall. Then he began caressing her again, falling into a rhythm as rhythmic as a clock. As rhythmic as if he hadn't heard her at all. They didn't say anything more.

I remembered how my mother had pushed the leaf

85

in the birdbath, and other moments, when she'd pause to let the soil run out between her fingers while gardening, moments I'd never dared to name. And I'd never imagined that she'd dare to name them herself. I don't think she could have if it hadn't been in the dark. I rolled over so that I faced away from them, pretending that I too hadn't heard.

LATER, I WOKE to the sound of someone coming down the stairs. The screen door gently squeaked shut. I sat up to look out the window. It was Meg. She was carrying a blanket.

I slipped into my jeans and sweatshirt. I followed Meg at a distance, staying close to the edge of the dirt road so that she couldn't see me. Chris was waiting for her, sitting on a tree stump. He kissed Meg and then, taking her hand, led her into the woods.

Crouching behind a tree, I waited until the beam of their flashlights became still. I crawled just close enough so that I could see where they'd spread the blanket out. They kissed again. She lay down so that her head was in his lap.

I imagined how he must be stroking her hair. But then he said, "Oh, yeah, that's it. Just like that. You're so good."

She raised her head. "Tell me you love me."

He pushed her head back down. "You had it. Don't stop now. You don't know how good you are."

Quietly I crept out of the woods. I ran back to the house.

THE NEXT MORNING I went down to the lake for a swim even though it was a cloudy, cool day. Meg sat alone at the end of the dock. Her hands were burrowed deep in her sweatshirt pockets and she wore her hood up, tied so tightly around her face none of her curls showed. I was afraid that she had known all along that I'd followed her and now would say something. But all she said was, "It's cold. You really going in?"

I waded out until I was standing near the end of the dock. "It's not that cold."

Meg took one hand out of her sweatshirt to chip off a piece of flaking paint from the dock. "Leslie . . . do you think Chris is cute?"

It wasn't like her to care what I thought. "Yeah," I shrugged. "He's cute."

She dropped the chip into the water. The sunfish flocked around it, expecting the scraps Aunt Holly sometimes allowed us to feed them from our dinner plates. When they saw that there was nothing there, the sunfish swam away from the surface, seemed to become transparent and then entirely to fade except for the occasional glint of their scales. "Well, I think he's *real* cute," she said, burrowing her hands back into her sweatshirt.

I'd heard about that, what Meg had been doing to Chris in the woods. But I'd never actually *known* anyone to do it. And right now I just didn't want to know. I thought of Joanne peering into her book and thought that maybe she too didn't want to know. I dove in and swam out to the raft. When I looked back at Meg, she seemed to have completely folded in on herself, sitting cross-legged and leaning her elbows on her knees.

"You scared me," Joanne exclaimed when she saw me outside the porch. "What are you doing here?"

"I had nothing to do so I took the rowboat out," I said, climbing through the screen. "I hid it in the trees by the canoe."

Joanne sat in the same fold-up chair, with a book open on her lap.

"What are you reading now?" I asked.

"War and Peace."

"You finished *Moby-Dick* already?"

"No . . . it was kind of slow. This moves faster."

I peered into the kitchen and was surprised but somehow relieved to find that the blue cup was still there. When I turned to look back at Joanne, she was staring at me. She'd stared at me like that down at the beach when my mother had gotten up and walked away. Beginning to feel embarrassed all over again, I felt compelled to say, "My mother isn't always like that."

"Like what?"

"Like she was yesterday. She just gets upset some-times."

"I know," said Joanne, shrugging. "I was just won-dering, well . . ." Then she laughed. "I mean, do you *really* think my mother stole her toys?"

"Yeah, she might have."

Joanne just looked at me.

"I mean, when we were little we were taking each other's things all the time. That little black stallion with the adjustable saddle? That was mine but you always insisted it was yours."

"Yeah . . ."

I was pleased that there was nothing more she could think of to say to that. I looked back through the win-dow. "Don't you wonder about what's inside? What it's like in there?"

"Yeah, sure, I guess."

"Well . . . maybe we could find out."

"Oh, yeah?" Joanne laughed. "Since when have *you* become so big on breaking and entering?"

"It wouldn't really be like that—we wouldn't steal or anything, just look around." I opened the drawer with the pipes and tore off the lid to a pack of cards. I tried to slide the lid between the door and the latch.

"Aren't you supposed to be using a credit card or something?"

"This might work. It looks like just a stupid lock

anyway. Look at this keyhole. It's one of those old ones for antique keys."

But after a few more minutes of watching me struggle Joanne returned to her chair.

I didn't really expect that I could actually get the door unlocked. But I became obsessed with the idea, getting down on my knees so that I was at eye level. Joanne had long since become immersed in her book, absently twisting the fringe on her shorts, when the lid slipped into place. The door opened.

The buckling linoleum floor creaked as we tiptoed into the kitchen. We forgot ourselves as we began going through the cabinets. They were empty except for an open box of Raisin Bran, a bag of green noodles, soup cans, a jar of wheat germ and an assortment of blue plates. More blue cups hung from hooks beneath the cabinets. What I hadn't been able to see through the window was that the handles were braided like vines, their bases blossoming out into small clusters of leaves. On the counter tucked between yellow canisters of flour and sugar was a vase filled with what I thought at first glance were plastic flowers. They were small pinwheels. When we blew on them, their stripes blurred into rainbows.

We found more fish skulls in the living room, tiny ones as if from sunfish or even minnows. Or maybe they were from fish that had died in his tank. It occurred to

me then that he had collected the skulls simply because
he liked them. Maybe he had even thought they were
beautiful. They were arranged in little clusters along the
windowsills, as my mother had arranged her ceramic
chickadees along our sills at home.

There was a green velvet chair and couch, their seats
worn down to gray patches. Next to the couch was a
driftwood lamp that was also a table, its trunk passing
through a round slab of wood. "Oh, *look*, Leslie," Joanne
exclaimed, turning on the lamp. Its shade was decorated
with sea gulls that seemed to be actually flying; their
wings were cut out so that they were three-dimensional.

I thought about how long it probably had been
since that lamp was turned on, with only the sun feeling
its way through the house like fingers. The lamp, the
green couch and chair, the blue cups and fish skulls, all
seemed so fixed they existed in their own right. For us
they held no meaning beyond what we were willing to
imagine.

And watching the gulls sail around and around as
Joanne slowly spun the shade, I remembered something
I'd nearly forgotten—we could imagine just about anything we wanted. We could transport ourselves that way,
as we used to when we'd pretend. When we knew how
to live entirely within the moment, and the moments
were these wonderful little capsules. I'd never thought
those capsules would burst, leaving me to feel like I felt

now—as afraid as I had felt watching my father motor off across the lake.

"We should look for pictures of this man," said Joanne. "Maybe in the bedroom."

"No, we shouldn't."

"Why not?"

"Because. It's teatime."

"What?"

"Let's make tea."

She smiled.

We didn't look to see if there were any real tea bags. Neither of us liked tea. We were content to sip from empty blue cups as we sat at the kitchen table and gazed out at the trees. I don't think that we were pretending to be anyone in particular. We just weren't ourselves.

FIVE

Y ou'll like Addie," said my
mother, grating an orange rind. The ends of her hair
were wrapped around small pink rollers and she wore
her spring bathrobe, the one with pockets outlined in
the shape of apples. It was Saturday morning and I was
pouring myself a bowl of cereal.

She'd met Addie through our church. My father had
been encouraging her to sign up to do some volunteer
work ever since the "scene" she'd made at Indian Lake.
Besides, he was concerned about her spending too much
time alone in the house.

Addie was short for Adelaide and tomorrow was
her eighty-ninth birthday. My mother was making her
an orange cake—Addie loved oranges. When she visited

Addie every afternoon, she took a plate of sectioned oranges for them to share while they watched the birds. She'd bought a feeder for Addie's living room window.

My mother put aside the now bald orange. "She has a great spirit, a spirit all her own. A spirit that rises up from *inside* her." She cracked three eggs and separated their yolks. "If it's allowed to." She beat the yolks briskly. "If Claire didn't treat her so much like a child."

Claire was the woman who took care of Addie. My mother believed it was because of her that Addie was "slipping."

"She sounds great," I said, trying to sound enthusiastic, even though I had no intention of liking Addie. It was enough having to sit through church on Sundays, trying to keep my thoughts from wandering during my prayers, without having to spend Sunday afternoon with a dreary old lady.

But I was glad my mother had found someone besides me to throw a party for. When I had parties now, they were sleep-overs, and at the last one she'd draped herself in a sheet and appeared at the living room door while we were playing levitation. She'd held a flashlight under her chin so that she really did look ghostly, and my friends had squealed delightedly. They all seemed to love her as much as they used to, when she'd been known for giving the best birthday and end-of-school parties around. But I was embarrassed by her now, by all the attention she still showed me—other mothers would have disappeared upstairs to watch TV. When she'd seen how I was the only one not laughing, she'd pulled off the sheet. She'd folded it as she would have taking it out of the dryer.

I knew my father was glad, too, that my mother had found Addie; she no longer fretted·so much about all the time he spent in his study. He'd complain about the "long hours" he had to put into teaching, how he wasn't able to devote more of himself to his writing. At the same time, he hoped to become chairman of the department and would take on extra time-consuming projects like the college literary magazine. He rushed around so now, as if he were always late getting somewhere.

He came into the kitchen as my mother was taking the cake out of the oven. "That smells *delicious*," he said, pouring himself a cup of coffee. He stood there drinking it quickly, as he would before he'd rush off to class, even though there wasn't anywhere he had to be today.

My mother looked at us then, saying, "I wouldn't ask you both to come, but there just isn't anyone else. Except that son of hers who hardly ever calls. I hope he sends her flowers at least." She sat down at the table and began taking the rollers out of her hair, lining them up in a neat row. "Who knows. You might actually enjoy yourselves." For a moment she looked eagerly up at my father. "She was a great pianist once. You've always been interested in musicians."

"She sounds great," said my father, kissing the top

of her head. "I just wish . . . well, she was a little closer in age."

"You wish I had more friends."

My father blew on his coffee.

She rotated the cake, examining it lovingly. "Addie *is* a friend."

FROM WHAT MY mother had told me about Claire, I wasn't prepared to like her, imagining her as a large, brusque woman. Instead, she was half the height of my mother and only slightly plump. Her features were small, her eyes pressed into her face like raisins. She wore her graying hair back in a tarnished butterfly barrette. "Welcome," she said in a cheerful, soothing voice as she led us down a short hall.

"Did Addie's son call?" asked my mother.

"This morning. And he sent her the most beautiful lilies."

"Oh. Well, that's good," said my mother, sounding surprised and a little disappointed. "Well, let me just drop these things off in the kitchen." Along with the cake, she also left the bag of presents on the counter. She would bring the presents in later, after she'd had a chance to make sure the wrappings hadn't become crumpled or torn in transit.

In the living room, sunlight fell thickly through yellowed lace curtains, across a worn oriental rug. Needlepoint pillows of red barns, lakes, and mountains lined a green couch. Above the couch hung a portrait of a young girl holding a squirrel. She was pouting as if about to cry.

The room smelled like sour sponges. My father rubbed his nose. My mother didn't seem to notice the smell as she breezed across to where Addie sat slumped in a wheelchair. She leaned over to kiss her cheek. "Happy birthday, Addie."

Addie seemed to be staring at a spot on the rug, her mouth hanging partly open. Over a dress of blue scallop shells she wore a gray shawl, the gray of wet newspapers. Her face was covered with moles and her legs were swollen so that she seemed not to have ankles. Except for a few scattered white curls, she was bald. Her scalp shone like the belly of a fish.

"What's this?" asked my mother, picking up a bear that sat on the metal tray of Addie's wheelchair.

"That was my present," said Claire.

My mother looked at her accusingly.

"She saw it on television, Mrs. Flynn, said she wanted one." Claire adjusted Addie's shawl. "You enjoy yourself now, sweetheart. I'll be just in the next room if you need me."

I sat on the couch and was glad that my father sat next to me. I'd begun to see that he really was as handsome as my mother had always said, and I was proud of the way he could make my girlfriends giggle when he drove us to the ice-skating rink. He'd tell them that he was "in heaven surrounded by so many pretty women." They'd watch enviously as he gently pinched my cheek good-bye, imagining that we were actually very close.

When Claire had left, my mother asked, pulling up a chair, "So how has your birthday been so far?"

Addie continued to stare at the rug. A bead of drool hung from the corner of her mouth.

My mother stood up, spread her feet apart in front of the wheelchair and cupped her hands under Addie's armpits so that she could pull her upright. "Happy *birthday*, Addie," she repeated.

Addie didn't seem quite so small now that she no longer slouched. She lifted her hands to my mother's face. "Marion . . ."

"Yes, Addie, it's me," said my mother, sounding relieved. "And I'd like you to meet my family."

Addie stared at me. Her eyes melted behind her thick glasses. "Oh," she sighed. "An angel."

My mother laughed. "Well, maybe sometimes, Addie. Not all the time."

Addie smiled, her tongue sticking out between her lips. "I bet you'd like to wear gold shoes."

My mother nodded at me.

"Yes . . ." I said uncertainly.

Addie looked pleased. "*I* wanted to wear gold shoes."

My mother abruptly stood up. "I'll be right back," she said excitedly, "with some surprises."

She left us alone with Addie. My father cleared his throat, glancing at his watch. He tapped his foot as he would now at dinner when he was anxious to get back to his study. "My wife tells me you were quite a pianist."

"A what?"

"Pianist. You played the piano."

Addie spread her fingers out across the tray. Her nails were yellow. "I was good, yes. Mozart, always Mozart."

"Did you play professionally?"

Addie just looked at him.

"Did you play in concert halls?"

"I played for my *parents*," said Addie, sounding annoyed. "I wore red velvet dresses at Christmas and played for my parents."

"I see," said my father, shifting so that he sat with his feet together and arms pressed against his sides as he used to sit in the too-small chairs during conferences with my grade school teachers. He looked toward the window where my mother had hooked the feeder onto its ledge. There were no birds.

I couldn't think of anything to say and resented that I felt I had to say anything at all. I was somehow reminded too much of myself, of how I thought others

saw me, tall and skinny, still undeveloped. I often wondered whether it showed, that I had never really kissed
a boy. So that I wouldn't have to look at Addie, I picked
up the glass paperweight beside me on the end table.
Orange and red ladybugs were suspended inside.

My mother returned with the presents. "Look what
we have for you," she said, arranging them on Addie's
tray.

"Oh!" exclaimed Addie hoarsely.

"Go ahead and open them."

Addie pulled out the ends of the ribbon so that they
snapped back into curls. She did this repeatedly until
my mother helped her slide the ribbon off.

From the shape of the box, I hadn't expected the
present to be two bottles of bath oil. Addie made fists
around the caps, silver balls. My mother gently took
them from her and held them so that Addie would have
to look at the labels. "They're Jean Naté."

Addie stared blankly.

"They'll make your skin feel smooth as silk," said
my mother, handing the bottles to my father to look at.
He weighed them on his palms.

There was a bow rather than a ribbon on the second
present. Addie flattened it with her palm to watch it
pop up again. My mother pulled it off and stuck it onto
Addie's breast pocket. "There. Don't you look pretty.
Now, why don't I just help you, I Scotch-taped this too

tightly maybe," she said, already sliding her nails quickly along each side. She unwrapped it enough so that all Addie had to do was pull back the paper. My mother lifted the lid of a slender box and held up two handkerchiefs.

"Look, Addie." She pointed to the corners where she had embroidered Addie's initials.

Addie gazed at them distantly, caressing the bow on her pocket.

My mother slowly refolded the handkerchiefs. "Well, I thought you might need new ones."

"Can I see?" asked my father.

She shrugged, handing them to him.

In the next moment Addie had taken the bow off her blouse and stuck it on her head. She grinned at me. She grinned so broadly I could see that all her front teeth were missing except for two—she looked like a walrus. I couldn't help laughing. It felt so good to laugh.

"Leslie," my mother snapped.

I smiled down at the floor.

"That's going to hurt, you know," my mother said, turning to Addie. "When you have to take it off."

Addie still grinned. "I'll wear it to my grave then."

I started to laugh again.

My mother glared at me. "Leslie, you come with me."

As we left the room, I heard my father clear his

throat again. He'd kept his hand over his mouth to hide his own smile. "It's a beautiful day, isn't it?"

"You know, it's not nice to laugh at people," my mother whispered angrily as we entered the kitchen.

"*She* was laughing."

"I don't care. It's still not nice."

She began going through the cabinets, snapping them open and closed noisily. She brushed past Claire, who stood at the sink doing a few dishes.

"Can I help you find something?" Claire asked.

"Dessert plates."

Claire opened the one cabinet my mother had missed. "I guess you need forks too. And napkins."

"I brought napkins. Party napkins. I wouldn't think of using regular napkins for a party."

Claire sighed. "Fine."

My mother opened the freezer for the ice cream. "When was the last time this was defrosted?"

"It ices up quickly."

"Then you should have someone in to look at it, don't you think?"

"It works fine. It's just old."

"Then she should have a new one."

"Mrs. Flynn . . ." Claire frowned, turning back to the sink. "I really do just take care of her fine."

My mother shut the refrigerator. She swung the ice

cream carton in its freezer bag. "I know," she said quietly. She handed me a package of birthday candles.

"How many?" I asked.

"Oh, I don't know. Just enough to go around."

"You mind if I join you all?" asked Claire.

"Join us? Why, of course not," my mother stumbled. "There's plenty of cake."

We sang "Happy Birthday" as we filed back out to the living room. My mother placed the cake on Addie's tray. Addie gripped the arms of her chair. The candles flickered in her glasses.

"It's orange, Addie, your favorite," said my mother. "Orange sponge cake."

"Orange?" Addie groped toward her. "Marion. You're so good to me."

My mother straightened one of the candles.

"Well, Addie, aren't you going to make a wish?" Claire asked.

"Why, yes," said Addie. "And I know what I wish." She breathed in deeply and managed to blow out all the candles.

"Tell us what you wished," said my mother.

"It won't come true then, will it?" said Claire.

My mother ignored her. She leaned over, bringing her face close to Addie's. She stroked her cheek. "Tell us what you wished, Addie."

Addie shrugged. "I wished to die, of course."

My father shifted, rearranging the pillows behind him.

My mother sat down heavily. "That's a terrible wish, Addie."

Addie chuckled. "But I do, dear."

My mother stared at the coffee table where she'd set up the plates and forks. Balloons floated up from each corner of the napkins.

"Do you know what's over there, on the other side?" Addie leaned over as far as she could, so that she could touch my mother's knee. "Nothing. A cool calm lake of pure nothing."

My mother gently removed Addie's hand from her knee. "We forgot something," she barely whispered. "We forgot something to drink."

"I can get it," Claire said.

My mother left the room as if she hadn't heard Claire.

Addie shook her head at the cake. She'd sunk back down in her chair. Claire pulled Addie's shawl around her shoulders as gently as if trying not to disturb her.

"Cut the cake," I said.

Addie blinked at me.

"Cut the *cake*."

"It's all right," said my mother. She was suddenly there behind me, resting her hand on my shoulder.

I thought she'd fold Addie's fingers around the cake

knife like she used to fold mine. But she cut the cake herself. I handed around the plates after she had scooped balls of ice cream onto each slice.

When we were finished and my mother was clearing away Addie's plate, she asked, "You liked the cake, didn't you, Addie?"

Addie nodded. The bow now drooped to one side.

"And you liked your presents?"

"I have to go."

"Go?"

"To the bathroom," said Claire, already removing the tray and turning the chair toward the door. "And I think she'll be ready for a nap after this. Don't you think so, Addie?"

Addie stared at the floor.

In the next moment she was gone. My mother gathered up the wrappings, folding them neatly. She looked out at the empty feeder. "We should put seed out before we leave," she said distantly.

ADDIE DID DIE soon after that. Claire called one morning to tell us she had "gone peacefully in her sleep."

"No one dies peacefully in their sleep," said my mother, looking out the kitchen window and clawing the inside of her apple pockets. "No one dies peacefully alone."

My father had not yet gone to work. He walked up

behind her and wrapped his arms around her. "I'm sorry. I know how much she meant to you."

She leaned back against him. "I don't think you do."

WHEN I CAME home after gymnastics practice that day, I found my mother sitting in their rocking chair sorting through my father's cuff links. She'd placed the ones she'd matched on the windowsill.

"Is it that time already?" she asked, looking at her wrist. She rubbed where she'd forgotten to put on her watch. She was still in her bathrobe.

"Why aren't you dressed?"

She looked out the window. "Well, I've just been thinking. Because, you know, Addie's not at all over there, on that side. She's right here with us now. She's in everything that moves. She's in the breeze rustling those leaves."

The way she sat there reminded me of the way she had sat alone at a faculty barbecue recently, picking the seeds out of a watermelon slice, while my father and I played softball. "You knew she was going to die," I said.

She looked at me.

I shrugged. "She was old."

She paired up the last of the links and smoothed out her now empty lap. "We're like strangers now, aren't we?"

"What?"

BLUE GLASS

"You used to want to be just like me, remember that? You'd even sneak into my drawers and try on my stockings and scarves."

"Why are you talking like this?"

"Because." She leaned forward then so that her robe fell away. I could see the blue of a vein inside her thigh. Her face was contorted horribly, as if she were experiencing some kind of physical pain. "I need you."

I saw then more clearly than I ever had before just how lonely she really was. But I couldn't stand to see her sitting there like that, her feet turned in and her hands hanging limply between her legs as if she were a cripple. "Why can't you just be my mother? You're supposed to be my *mother!*"

I ran downstairs and out into the yard. I did something I hadn't done in years, climbed the maple tree by the side of the garage.

I heard my mother calling for me. Calling that she was sorry, so sorry, calling for all the neighbors to hear. Part of me wanted to answer her, that part of me that was remembering how she had been able to enlarge my world with the smallest things, marveling at the gold-rimmed wings of moths or the rainbows arcing through the sprinkler's spray. I didn't answer. And after a few minutes she went inside, probably assuming I'd gone to a friend's house.

I'd snagged the hem of my new skirt and scuffed

107

my white boots, and I was disgusted with myself for being up in that tree at all. But I stayed there until my father came home, peeling off the bark and chipping my nail polish. When he finally drove up, I climbed down and ran to him as I hadn't since I was seven or eight. As I used to run only to my mother.

SIX

One day the summer of my freshman year, I was sitting on my grandparents' front steps watching my grandmother stuff Juicy Fruit gum and chocolate-covered laxative pills down mole holes. She'd read that this worked, as she had read somewhere that beer killed slugs. Every morning there were at least a dozen slugs floating in each of the old tuna fish cans she'd scattered throughout her flower garden.

My mother sat at the porch table in front of an easel the size of a plate stand. She was teaching herself to paint miniature landscapes from photographs. After Addie, my father had encouraged her to get involved in something else, something like fund-raising this time, because she had too much time on her hands. "I have plenty to do," she'd said. "There's plenty to do around here. Like picking up after you. I've never had to pick up after Leslie like I do after you."

There was nothing my father could have said to that. For a while he tried to improve, but dropping his things around the house was as subconscious as the way he'd run his fingers back and forth along the part in his hair while reading.

To soften the gum, Gramma June folded the sticks into her mouth. "I don't know how you kids stand this stuff," she said, sticking out a piece between her teeth. "It's sickly sweet."

"It's not fattening," I said.

"Aren't they going to smell your scent?" my mother asked, her paintbrush poised in the air.

Gramma June rolled the gum between two fingers. "Well, I hadn't thought of that."

"They're practically blind, aren't they? Their sense of smell must be twice as strong."

Gramma June frowned. She leaned down to stuff the gum into a hole. "Oh, they're not that smart."

My mother dabbed at her small canvas.

"Where's Grampa Cole?" I asked.

"He's gone up for the mail," said my grandmother, walking to the edge of the lawn. She looked up the street. Every day she worried that my grandfather would forget his way home. He could remember when he was six and used to crawl under the piano to play with the pedals while his sister practiced. And he could still remember to feed the chickens and lock them into the coop at night, but he no longer could tell the difference between the dishwasher and the refrigerator.

I looked down at my shoes. They were blue plastic moccasins. Sequin stars floated in the toes. I shifted my feet so that the stars drifted away from each other. If only it were Friday, my father would be driving out. I'd wait for him at the edge of the lawn, sitting cross-legged in my favorite yellow sundress.

"What are you thinking so hard about?" asked my mother.

I forced myself to look up from my shoes. "Nothing."

She pressed down the corners of the photograph. It was a picture of that inlet where she used to help me collect hermit crabs in my sand bucket. "Oh, you must be thinking about *something*."

I didn't answer her, looking back down at my shoes.

"Oh, *there* he is," Gramma June exclaimed. My grandfather walked slowly up the driveway as if balancing himself along an invisible line. His white fishing hat was pressed down on his head like a bonnet.

Grampa Cole handed her the mail. "Nothing personal," he said, taking a package of coupons for himself. He sat in one of the wicker chairs and opened the package. He set up the coupons on his knees like playing cards.

I stood up, shaking out my skirt.

My mother noisily tinkled her brush in her saucer of water. "Where are you off to?"

"Just a bike ride."

She got up and took my place on the steps, gathering up the gum wrappers Gramma June had piled there. She peered at them as I'd once seen her peer down at a wounded finch she'd tried to save. "You're always disappearing."

"I'll be back soon, Mom."

As I rode away, she called, "Be careful of your skirt. It might get caught in the spokes!"

I pedaled fast so that I could feel the wind. I hated how my mother made me feel guilty for wanting to be alone. If I wasn't riding my bike, I was escaping to my room in my grandparents' house, where I'd fantasize about kissing men who liked to take me for walks through moonlit fields. For the most part these men were imagined, but sometimes it was Todd Curtis from school. He had a girlfriend, but he was someone I'd liked ever since we were in the same art class. At the moment when Todd was seducing me into the grass, I would be complete. I would have a full bust line instead of breasts that disappeared whenever I lay down.

But my mother would come in and I'd have to throw

open a magazine. She'd ask if she could take down my curtains to wash them. Or she'd bring me a vase of black-eyed Susans freshly cut from the garden. Placing the vase in my window, she'd run her finger across the sill. She'd insist that my room needed a good dusting, that it would take her only a minute. Then she promised to leave me alone.

One day when she brought me a glass of iced tea, she sat on the footstool tucked beside my dresser. I used to stand on it to reach the sink. She sat so close to the floor her knees nearly met her chin. "I was wondering, have you noticed anything . . . different about your father?"

I pulled myself up on my bed, closing my magazine. "Different? Like what?"

"I don't know exactly . . ." she ran her fingers around the toes of her sandals.

"Have *you*?"

She looked toward the window. "No. Not really." Then she stood up and leaned on my dresser, looking in the mirror. "It's just that . . . well, he always had this special way of . . . looking at me."

She worried now that if my father no longer loved her, it was because he no longer found her attractive. At the same time, she seemed to be doing less and less to make herself attractive. She never wore her hair down anymore, but tightly pulled back into a false bun. At night she kept it hidden in a drawer beside their bed; my father couldn't stand to see it lying on their bureau. I loved best how she used to wear her hair pulled back loosely, softly, with combs. The combs were always decorative, with starlike blue flowers or rhinestones so tiny they were splashes of light. They were among the things that had always fascinated me about her, like the leaves and roses she'd embroidered on her blouses and skirt hems.

Now she wore an old sundress that looked too small for her, the cloth belt riding above her waist. Its pink had faded to a watery salmon and what was left of the embroidery around the collar was torn green threads. I could just see half of her face reflected in my mirror. Her features were erased by the gray window light. "Daddy loves you, Mom."

She looked at me. "You think so?"

"God, Mom."

"I know, I know." She began straightening my dresser, piling my loose earrings into the old Easter basket where I kept my jewelry. "Well, I won't bother you anymore."

I picked up my magazine.

She tiptoed out of my room even though it was carpeted.

I PARKED MY bike in front of the drugstore—I loved to browse through the cosmetic section, enjoying the way the powders were encased in clear plastic domes. Sometimes I'd buy something like a strawberry-flavored lip gloss, but for the most part I was content just to look.

I was examining a set of eye shadows when Chip came over to me. We both worked part-time at the Farmer's Market, although I'd never talked to him; I worked behind the deli counter, while he was always somewhere else, stocking shelves or bagging bagels. I had never even thought to talk to him, maybe because he was too much sought after by all the other girls behind the counter. He had brown eyes, a compact build and hair just long enough to be sexy, not hippy.

"First time I've seen you around town," he said. He dropped some change into the breast pocket of his jeans jacket, having just bought a pack of cigarettes. Sometimes at work when I was taking out the garbage, he'd be smoking, sitting on a crate behind the kitchen.

"I ride my bike up sometimes," I said, embarrassed that we were standing in front of the cosmetics.

He began opening the cigarettes, unwinding the blue strip from around the cellophane as delicately as if it were a surgical procedure. "I guess you don't live around here," he said. "I mean, I haven't seen you around school."

"I just come here for the summers—my grandparents live a couple of blocks away."

He nodded, slipping the pack into his jacket pocket after taking out a cigarette, and I thought he'd probably leave then. But he continued to stand there, now rubbing one finger back and forth under his chin. He already had whiskers, something I hadn't noticed before. "So you like working at the market?"

"Yeah, it's great."

"I guess," he laughed. "I've already been there three summers now. This is my last, though—next year I'll be out of school, working at a real job."

"You going to stay around here?"

"For a while," he shrugged. "I may go back to school eventually, but I've had enough of all that for a while. How old are you anyway?"

"How old am I? Fifteen," I blurted, before I could think to lie.

"Really?"

"Why?"

"I don't know," he said, shifting from one foot to the other. "You seemed a little . . . older." He looked at me, his eyes slowly traveling down my front until they landed at my moccasins. "Nice shoes," he laughed.

"Thanks," I said, wishing I wasn't still holding that eye shadow. "Well, I should probably get going."

"Yeah, well, me too," he said, for a moment gently tugging on a bag of cotton balls that hung on a rack next to him. He was really rather short, but he seemed tall to me now. "See you at work."

I was sorry I hadn't lied about my age, even though

I wasn't sure I even liked him. But after that he sometimes visited me in the deli section, leaning on the
counter as he rotated the glass lids on jars of Gummi
bears and olives. I liked how he would look at me, like
he had in the drugstore—in a way I'd never been looked
at before.

ONE PARTICULARLY HOT day Gramma June decided that
she wanted to get out her wedding china from the attic.
She'd packed it away a few years ago, having bought a
set of large hand-glazed ceramic plates.

"Why all of a sudden do you want to get out your
wedding china?" asked my mother, as the three of us
climbed the attic stairs. Grampa Cole had gone up for
the mail.

"Does there have to be a reason?" Gramma June
asked. "Goodness, you can hardly move up here," she
said, grabbing onto an old laundry rack as she tried to
make her way between toaster ovens, sewing machines,
waffle irons and—a more recent acquisition—a rusted
wok. She lightly kicked a porcelain bedpan. "We could
make a planter out of that."

"You could make a planter out of a lot of things up
here," I said, noticing a foot warmer and a wooden
bucket. There were also floor lamps that no longer
worked but that I remembered from when I was little,
when Grampa Cole would try to fix them himself. He'd

also tried to fix their radio, the large old one that looked like a jukebox. It now lay on its side with a tangle of wires exposed.

I pulled boxes out from under the eaves, looking for the one marked "Wedding." My mother and Gramma June sat next to each other on the piano bench with the shredded seat cushion, opening each box and rustling through the newspapers.

"Oh, look," my mother cooed, holding up a ceramic Christmas tree. There were holes in the branches for candles. "We used to keep this on the mantel and light it on Christmas Eve, remember?"

"Yes, and it nearly burned the house down," said Gramma June. "Those little birthday candles you're supposed to stick in there burned down so quick they set the greens on fire."

My mother repacked the tree.

"Look at these," said Gramma June, picking out a pair of salt and pepper shakers. They were in the shape of Siamese cats that sat tall and primly, with blue rhinestones for eyes. "Cole gave these to me one anniversary. Can you imagine?"

"Oh, but they're so cute," said my mother. "Look at their pretty eyes." She set them on top of a lopsided washstand so that they were facing each other.

"I guess they are, aren't they," said Gramma June. She ran a finger along their tails that curled around their front paws. "And he was so proud. He never knew how to buy me what I really wanted. But he always tried. He was always so proud."

I could imagine Grampa Cole falling in love with the cats, believing that Gramma June would fall in love with them too. And I knew that even though they'd wound up in the attic, at the time Gramma June had been grateful; I remembered that she had actually used them, at least until their ears chipped and she had an excuse to put them away.

Finally I pulled out the right box.

"Oh, I'd forgotten how pretty they are," Gramma June exclaimed, holding up a plate. "I'd forgotten how much I loved this pattern." She hugged the plate to her chest. "Oh, how could I have ever wanted to put these away?"

"You've always done that, Gramma June," I said. "Putting stuff away for a while, then taking it out again."

"I suppose," said Gramma June distantly. "No, I remember. It was just before Cole retired. And I remember . . . I remember being afraid of that. I wanted it to be like a beginning for us. I wanted something new. I even thought about moving. Somewhere warm. Somewhere where winters weren't so gray."

"I thought you loved it here," said my mother, sounding hurt.

"I did." Gramma June sighed, lowering the plate

back into the box. It was rimmed with tiny gold bells. "I do." She looked at the cats again. "I wouldn't think of moving now."

We all sat there for a moment longer, until my grandmother looked at her watch. "Cole should be back by now. I didn't hear him come in, did you?" Before we could answer, she was already hurrying down the stairs.

"So many things," my mother said wistfully. "So many forgotten things."

I suddenly felt homesick. Not for our house back home, not even for the way things used to be before my grandfather had begun to forget. But for something in myself, for that something that I'd begun to hope and believe was there. That something that was all me, not my grandmother, not my mother. "It's too hot up here," I said, getting up. As I went downstairs I could hear my mother opening another box.

ONE SUNDAY AT the beach, I was burying my father's foot when Chip came over. I stood up abruptly, embarrassed that I must have looked like a child playing in the sand. "We work together at the market," I said, quickly introducing him.

My mother and grandmother nodded from the shadows of their umbrella. Grampa Cole waved to us from his fold-up chair as if we stood at a great distance.

"Looks like a good surf today," said my father. "Been in yet?"

"A while ago," said Chip. "I was getting ready to go in again."

My mother ran her finger back and forth along her collarbone.

"Are you here just for the summer too?" asked my father.

"No, I live here, just a few blocks away."

He wore a skimpy black and white bathing suit that revealed more shape down there than I had imagined. He turned to me and nodded toward the ocean. "Want to go in?"

"Stay in front of the lifeguard," my mother yelled as we ran into the water.

WE LINGERED ON the crest of the waves, drifting toward each other until our feet touched.

"What if I was a shark?" Chip asked. "What if I wanted to eat you?"

I found myself smiling, trying not to smile. "I wouldn't let you."

Chip dove under me. His hands reached for my legs. I squealed and rode the next wave in. He coasted in behind me.

I ran up the beach. Chip grabbed me around my waist and buried his face in my neck. "I got you now," he whispered. Our breathing slowed. We stood like that for what seemed a long time.

"Come back and sit with us for a while," Chip said.

"Who's us?"

"A couple of friends, that's all."

"I have to tell my parents first." When he started to follow me, I said, "I'll meet you there."

As I APPROACHED my family, my mother beckoned to me from under the umbrella. I leaned over her. Her mouth was set into a line so thin and hard it could have been carved out of stone. "I wish you wouldn't do that. Prance up and down the beach like that."

"Prance?"

"You were making a spectacle of yourself."

"She's all right, Marion," said my father.

"But what must that boy think?"

I ignored her, looking at my father. "Chip asked me to join him."

"Go ahead," he said. "Just be home for dinner."

"How can you say that?" She'd moved to the edge of her seat. "She's too young for this kind of thing."

"What kind of thing, Mom? What do you think, that I can get pregnant from swimming with a guy?"

"This is getting unpleasant," said Gramma June.

"*She's* making it unpleasant," I said. "She's doing this, she always is."

My mother's face suddenly seemed to crumble. "You

sound like you hate me. How can you sound like you hate me?"

"Why do you have to ask such stupid questions?"

She only stared at me, her lips now seeming to fold in on themselves like a very old woman's.

"All right, you really want an answer? Because you *make* me hate you. I hate you, okay? I really hate you!" I grabbed up my towel and ran down the beach to Chip. And as I ran, I felt that I really did hate her. That I'd be perfectly happy never having to see her again.

As the afternoon wore on, Chip's friends began to leave the beach. When we were the only ones left, we had nothing to say to each other. I lay back and closed my eyes. "Sun feels great."

"Yeah."

Chip lay back beside me.

"It's getting late but it's still hot."

"Yeah."

He rested his hand on my stomach. His fingers moved in tiny circles that grew into bigger ones. "You're beautiful, you know."

"Beautiful?"

"Yeah. I love watching you." His tongue pried open my lips and filled my mouth. I forced it out.

"You've never kissed anyone before, have you?" he said.

"Not really." I looked down at his chest. My eyes

traveled farther down his body, to the bulge in his crotch.

"And you've never seen one of those."

If I had been staring that stupidly in my fantasies, I would have been mortified. But this wasn't a fantasy. It was nowhere near as perfect. It was happening in a way I hadn't expected and I felt only mildly curious. And careless. A grin spread across my face like a rash.

"You can touch it if you want." Chip pulled me onto his towel and draped mine over us. It was late. The beach was almost empty. He guided my hand into his suit and I tried to hide my surprise as I felt him—he was strangely furrowed, not nearly as smooth as I'd imagined. I fingered him timidly, as if I had my hand down some animal's dark hole.

He forced my mouth open again and I tried to relax, letting his tongue wander over my gums. But I found myself thinking about my mother, how she was at my father now as much as she was at me. One Friday night after my grandparents and I had gone to bed, I came downstairs for a magazine I'd left in the living room. "You're driving me crazy, Marion, you know that," I heard my father saying from the couch. My mother sat in his lap with her head on his shoulder. "But you did. You used to call me 'loins.' 'Tender loins.' You haven't called me that in years. Why haven't you called me that in years?"

I was angry with her for being like that, angry with

the thought of her popping into my head when she wasn't even around.

Kissing my ear, Chip whispered, "We can do it if you want." The ocean crashed behind us with a force I could feel through the sand. "It would be all right. I promise."

I wanted to say yes and for a moment thought I could, as Chip loomed above me, blocking out the entire sky. But then I remembered myself, like something for a moment misplaced, some dull but necessary thing like my watch I'd take off while studying in bed and lose beneath my sheets. I should have been home by now. I was surprised that no one had driven down to find me. If my father hadn't been there, my mother probably would have.

MY FAMILY WAS finishing their dinner on the porch. They were eating off of the wedding china. Everyone looked up at me except for my mother.

"Your dinner's in the oven," my grandmother said.

It was spaghetti with meat sauce. The sauce was as watery as soup. My grandfather seemed to be the only one enjoying the meal, sucking strands of spaghetti off his fork. My grandmother had tucked a paper napkin under his chin.

I looked down at my own runny plate, thinking about Chip, how he had called me "beautiful." I'd always just thought of myself as too tall and too skinny. I remembered how unsure my fingers had been touching him and I had to look up. There was a full moon, transparent against a sky whose blue had not quite deepened. I wondered at how something so very far away could be seen at all.

The only sound was the clink of their silverware. "Isn't it amazing that you can see the moon?" I asked.

My mother looked at me for the first time.

My grandfather squinted at the sky. A piece of spaghetti hung from his lower lip. "It *is* something."

"Were you really at the beach all this time?" my mother asked.

"Let her be," my father said.

"Why are you always taking her side?"

"I'm not taking *sides*. I just think . . . you can crowd her, that's all."

"Is that why she hates me?"

"I don't hate you, Mom."

"You said you did."

"I was angry. You made me really angry."

"I'm just watching out for you. That's what I'm supposed to do, isn't it?"

"Watching out for me?" I laughed. "You're not allowing me to *breathe*."

She looked at my father. "How can you let her talk to me that way?"

My father adjusted his glasses. "Because I'm afraid she's right, sweetheart."

My mother traced the pattern of gold bells with a prong of her fork. "I'm just in everybody's way, aren't I?"

"Oh, Marion," sighed Gramma June.

"I know, I'm sorry. But it's true, Mother, isn't it? You know it's true. You know you do."

My father reached over to massage her neck. "Don't exaggerate."

She snapped her head around at him. "I don't exist for you anymore." Then she looked at me. "I don't exist for any of you anymore." She got up and began piling the plates with a tremendous clatter.

"Marion." My father took off his glasses to rub the bridge of his nose. "Just sit down for a minute."

"No. Because the fact is, I'm invisible. My own daughter can't even acknowledge my presence anymore. If she could, she'd walk right through me—"

"*Marion!*" yelled my father, yanking at the tablecloth. He yanked so hard all the water glasses spilled. A couple of the wedding plates crashed to the floor.

Gramma June clutched the arms of her chair. Grampa Cole repeatedly ran his hands over his napkin, flattening it against his chest. I sat completely still.

"What's happened to you?" asked my father, his face redder than I'd ever seen it. "What's happened to make you so impossible?"

My mother froze where she stood, gazing down at the water bleeding through the tablecloth.

"You exhaust me, Marion. You're exhausting this entire family. And not once do you ever stop to think about that, what you're doing to us, what you're doing to Leslie. Not once do you stop to think how *selfish* you've become."

She rested just the tips of her fingers on the edge of the table.

"You're not the woman I married, did you know that?"

She looked up then. She asked, as curiously as she would ask me about new friends I'd made at school, "What was she like? The woman you married?"

"What was she like?" He looked out across the lawn. "She was . . . gentle. She was trusting. Maybe too trusting. But she was so much easier to live with."

My mother looked out across the lawn too.

He sighed, now sounding only tired. "I'd better get going."

"What about dessert?" my mother asked faintly.

"Not tonight," he said, getting up as slowly as if he had to push himself up through some invisible surface. When he saw how Gramma June was staring down at her broken china, he went over to her. "I'm very sorry, June. I don't know what happened." He ran one hand through his hair. "And that scares me." He went inside.

My mother bent to pick up the pieces of the broken

plates. But she ended up sitting there, her legs folded to one side as she used to settle herself for a game of jacks with me, on the kitchen floor.

MY FATHER BARELY said good-bye to my mother that night, briefly kissing her cheek while she was doing the dishes. She didn't stand in the driveway with me like she usually would.

I got into the car and sat beside him. "I'm coming with you."

He laughed. "In your bathing suit?"

"I'll change first."

He tousled my hair. "Don't be silly." He no longer seemed flushed, only terribly pale, even paler in the bluish evening light. "I didn't know the weekend would have to end like this. I just wish . . ." I waited for him to continue but he only stared through the windshield.

The seat was warm from the sun but I suddenly felt cold. "Daddy? Should I be worried about anything?"

His face loosened into a look of helplessness I'd never seen before. "I don't know."

I must have been shivering because he took my hands and rubbed them like he used to after peeling off my frozen mittens. "We're okay." His hands were as cold as mine.

I STOOD AT the edge of the road as he drove away, hoping that he could see me in his rearview mirror. In the car, for the first time I had seen him in a moment of weakness. In a way my mother, I felt, had never seen him.

When I turned to go inside, she was standing on the porch, an empty laundry basket under one arm. As I walked toward her she moved the basket so that she cradled it in front of her like something precious. She smiled sadly. "You love your father very much."

I had to look away. A thread dangled from her skirt, quivering in a breeze I couldn't feel. "So do you."

She nodded, looking into the basket as if down a well. "The dew's falling." She walked past me to the laundry line on the side of the house.

I found Gramma June wandering around the house with a wet rag scrubbing the doorknobs, something she usually did only while waiting for company. She was scrubbing the living room doorknob when I came in and sat beside Grampa Cole on the couch. He'd fallen asleep in front of the television.

"It's terrible that your father should be going home like that, so upset. It's just terrible. I don't know what's gotten into your mother."

I watched her for a moment, the way she looked at the knob as if into a crystal ball, as if expecting to see something appear there. "What was she like, Gramma June, when she was little?"

"Your mother?" She shook out her rag. "Oh, she was so good. So sweet. Like your father said. She'd bring me things from school, things she made, little lopsided bowls—your Aunt Holly never brought me anything. Except once a bookmark, but I could tell she hardly put any effort into it, it was just something they all had to make, bookmarks. And all the time she gave me so much trouble, never coming right home from school—"

"I was asking about Mom."

"Oh . . . oh, dear."

I examined my nails, feeling oddly humiliated.

"I guess I was so busy keeping track of Holly that . . . well, Aunt Holly took so much *energy*, you know?"

"I know."

She looked at me. "I love your mother. You believe that, don't you?"

"Yes, Gramma June." But I was remembering something, the way my mother had sat opposite Gramma June and Aunt Holly at the kitchen table that one summer when Aunt Holly had come to visit. The way my mother had sat on her hands and the two of them seemed to have forgotten that she was there. I realized even more fully now than I had then just how starved my mother had always been for Gramma June's attention.

Gramma June came and sat on the arm of the couch. "Your mother *was* sweet." She looked toward the window. We could see where my mother was taking down the laundry. "And she had the biggest heart. I used to worry about that, the way she'd get so worked up over things, the birds that stunned themselves flying into the windows. I worried that her heart was too big." She shook her head. "I still worry."

My mother moved more slowly than usual, caressing each shirt as she folded it, and I thought about those lopsided bowls, how she had tried so hard to please Gramma June even back then. I suddenly longed for her to brush my hair, to feel her tugging on the knots so gently it never hurt. But for the first time I had a secret we couldn't share. The reality was, I could more easily tell my father about Chip than I could tell her. She plucked the empty line, watching it vibrate until it grew still.

"It's a face." My grandfather had woken up and was pointing at the fireplace.

I had to look for a long moment. But then I saw it—the two candlesticks at either end of the mantel were the eyes, the squat copper bowl in the middle, a nose. The mouth was the black hole leading up the chimney. Frozen open as if in a scream.

SEVEN

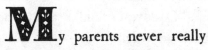y parents never really fought again after that summer. Instead, my father became very distracted. He would complain about barely being able to keep up with his work load, but when I'd pass by his study he'd be browsing through his bookshelf. "I'd forgotten what I had here," he once explained when he saw me standing there. Meanwhile, my mother would be downstairs moving very quietly back and forth between rooms. There would not even be the clatter of dishes as she was putting them away.

One Saturday afternoon when I got home from my friend Deirdre's house, my father was outside weeding the driveway, which surprised me; he hated to weed.

At the end of every summer, my mother and I would come home from Connecticut to find the place completely overgrown, with large sunflowers climbing up the side of the house. My mother would be so appalled she'd begin ripping up the weeds herself before she'd even gotten her bags inside.

My father was wheeling himself along the edge of our driveway on my old go-cart that he must have dug out from the very back of the garage. He tossed the weeds into the space where I used to put my feet, between the seat and where there had been a steering wheel with an orange horn. He was weeding so patiently it seemed to have become his favorite pastime.

"Daddy, it's fall," I said. "They're not going to grow back anyway."

"They'll grow back, they'll always grow back," he said. "Besides, it's still warm. We haven't had our Indian summer yet." He looked up for a moment, but not at me. He looked over at my mother's favorite tree, the crab apple that attracted so many of our birds. "And it gives me time to think."

"Think? Think about what?"

I thought he might reassure me as he had that night he'd driven away without saying good-bye to my mother. Shaking the earth off the roots of a dandelion, he only said, "I need to figure out a few things."

He reminded me of my grandfather then, the way

he seemed to crouch there like Grampa Cole would crouch in his chicken pen, as if he too were receding now into his own private sense of time and place. I went inside.

My mother was sitting at the kitchen table drinking tea. Usually when she had her tea, she'd flip through catalogues or cut out coupons. The table was empty.

"Have you two been fighting?" I asked, almost hopefully.

"You know we never fight anymore," she said, getting up. There was a time when on Saturday afternoons my father used to take her to the little shopping village that she loved and buy her something she didn't need, like copper pots she'd use for herb gardens. She placed her cup in the sink as quietly as if my father were still upstairs in his study. "We don't do anything anymore."

I went up to my room and sat on my bed, thinking that I had never heard my mother's voice sound so hollow. I could just hear the grate of the go-cart's wheels against the driveway's gravel and I felt strangely panicked. I pulled out all of my letters from Chip. We were never again alone as we had been at the beach, mostly because I didn't want to be; I was content with occasionally necking behind the market's kitchen. But he'd been writing me ever since I'd left, and I'd read and reread his letters because I liked to imagine myself as he saw me; in his eyes I wasn't so much skinny as "slim," and my long neck was "swanlike." I was "beautiful."

EXCEPT FOR WHEN I was reading his letters, I didn't think much about Chip. I was consumed by thoughts of Todd even though he was still going out with someone. Todd was now the art director for our annual school play, and he'd talked me into joining his stage crew to help paint the sets. "Just stay within the lines," he'd joked, when I reminded him of how bad I'd been in art. He himself had been the most talented in the class, able to abstract a still life into something vibrant and exciting, while the rest of us struggled to duplicate exactly the overripe fruit and wilted flowers.

He wasn't at all like Chip. Todd had tangled curly blond hair, the kind of young face that would never seem to need shaving and large hands and feet that sometimes would flail around like a puppet's. At the same time he seemed so much like a man, more brawny than small waisted like Chip. I liked how unrushed he always seemed, moving lazily back and forth across the stage, his tool belt sagging around his waist so that I could see the white band of his underwear. When he laughed, his eyes would widen, their blue becoming as ghostly as the blue of evening snow. I'd listen for that laugh when he was working where I couldn't see him, behind a flat or in the storeroom. I'd listen for the clink of the nails he carried around in the pockets of that tool belt.

But he'd only ever treated me as a kind of kid sister; in that art class he had teased me about the way I held my paintbrush, as if I were "drilling a hole," knowing that I was better than he was in math and science. When I was painting backstage, he sometimes would grab me from behind in a kind of bear hug and lift me off my feet so that I felt as young and weightless as a ten-year-old. As he was letting me go sometimes his hands would accidentally brush against my breasts.

TODD'S GIRLFRIEND, CAROLINE, was short and plump and had a wide smile that showed all her gums. She seemed to wear the same thing every day, a pair of patched jeans and a blue windbreaker. She wasn't involved in the play, too busy with the debate team and student government, but she'd drop by the theater every afternoon before going home. They'd sit for a while in the balcony where it was dark, and sometimes I'd glance up at them and could see him running his hand through her baby-thin hair.

"What do you think Todd sees in Caroline?" I asked Deirdre, when I was over there again one Saturday afternoon. As I lay on her bed I could hear one of her younger sisters downstairs in their rec room playing Ping-Pong with her friends. I liked that her house wasn't nearly as quiet as my own and I found myself spending more and more time there.

"Caroline? I don't know," she said, holding up one blouse after another as she emptied her closet. In a couple of weeks she would be giving a party for everyone involved in the play and she was already trying to decide what to wear. "He must be in love with her mind or something."

I had expected her to have more of an insight; Deirdre was comfortable around boys in a way that I wasn't, able at once to join them in a serious game of softball and to appear petite and fragile in her low-cut fuzzy sweaters and tight jeans. I knew that she'd had more than one chance to go all the way, but she was waiting for "just the right guy."

Deirdre sat down heavily beside me, in the middle of the pile of clothes. "I wish Katie didn't have to come. You know everyone's going to be fussing over her like *she's* giving the party instead of me."

Katie had gotten the lead while Deirdre had ended up with only a couple of lines in the final act. I hadn't tried out at all, the mere thought of an audition making my palms sweat.

"You shouldn't let her get to you so much," I said.

"Don't you see her at rehearsals?" she said, ignoring me. "She's always telling everyone else how to act—you'd think she was the director. And that's exactly how she's going to act at my party."

Two of Deirdre's front teeth were false, and when she worried like this, she would loosen their bridge with her tongue so that she could flick the teeth in and out, something I knew she did only in front of me. "They just never grew in," she'd explained apologetically when she'd first made me promise not to tell anyone, as she'd made me promise not to reveal that she straightened her hair and that she'd been thirty pounds heavier back in junior high school, when they'd been living in Philadelphia.

She'd moved here at the beginning of last year and had confided in me only when she realized that it didn't matter so much what I thought because I wasn't among the most popular girls at school. I kind of resented this, but I couldn't help liking Deirdre. I admired her for giving the party in the first place, for insisting on making herself noticed that way.

"Katie's not even that talented," I said. "She's pretty and cute and everyone has always loved her as far back as first grade. It's just that no one would have even thought to turn her down for the part."

"That's just *it*," said Deirdre, snapping her teeth back into place. "Why is that? Why is it that someone so completely talentless, so *brainless*, can end up so lucky?" She examined the collar on a blouse. "God, she's even got a great boyfriend—good-looking *and* intelligent."

"Yeah, but he doesn't have any style."

"Style?"

I rolled over onto my back and stared up at her ceiling where there was a rain leak in the shape of a cloud. "Like someone like Todd. He has style. He's not good-looking in an obvious way, but you remember him. Things about him."

Deirdre leaned over so that she could peer down into my face. "You like Todd," she said, grinning.

I had never talked to Deirdre about how I felt, mostly because I didn't think of Todd as a serious prospect, at least not as long as he was going out with Caroline. Besides, I wasn't sure she'd understand; Katie's boyfriend was much more her type. "I didn't say I liked him."

"You mention him enough."

I sat up and began shaking out her wrinkled blouses.

"You *do* like him," she said excitedly. "That's great."

"He's got a girlfriend, Deirdre. He and Caroline have been going out forever."

"So . . . ?"

"*So.*"

"You can have anyone you want," she said.

"I can?" I laughed.

"See? You don't even know it. Because you're just so shy all the time—at parties you're always standing against the wall where no one can see you. You're so pretty too, you don't even need makeup.'

"I wear makeup."

"Yeah, but you don't *need* to. You've got that great olive complexion, like you've never had a zit in your entire life. Dark-haired people are so lucky that way."

She moved over to her dollhouse. It was an enormous dollhouse, one she claimed never to have played with because the rooms were too large to fill with furniture. The roof was detachable, so now she used the rooms as storage for her makeup, jewelry and scarves. "You know, you don't know why he's still with Caroline. It might be just because no one better has come along," she said. "I mean, he must know that he's not exactly the kind of guy that girls will be lining up for, which is fine." She pulled out a bottle of perfume from one of the rooms. Instead of opening it, she held it up to admire its diamond shape. "The point is, you can't sit around and wait for him to come to you."

I DIDN'T LIKE the idea of having to go after Todd. On the other hand, Deirdre was probably right; if he never found out how much I liked him, why should he ever break up with Caroline?

The next time Todd came over to me, I was working in a corner of the stage by myself, painting the bricks on a folding screen he had designed as a fireplace. "You're going to be the world's best brick painter when you get done," he said, coming up behind me and lifting me up.

When he put me down, I leaned back against him. I held onto his arms that were still crossed around me, just shifting them so that his hands touched my breasts. For a moment he froze. Gradually his fingers began to stir, cautiously exploring.

Then I did what I never thought I'd have the nerve to do—I turned around and kissed him. His mouth felt cold and hard, as frozen as his fingers had been. I kissed him harder and he suddenly relaxed, grabbing my buttocks. Just as suddenly he let me go. "Jesus," he said, exhaling.

He started to walk off but then looked back at me. "Jesus," he repeated, sounding less startled now than amused, even pleased, which gave me a powerful boost of confidence.

"What about Him?" I asked.

He started to smile, and as if to hide it quickly turned away. He left me, walking a little less lazily than usual.

I COULDN'T BELIEVE it—I couldn't believe I'd actually been so bold as that, and I was feeling exhilarated when I got home that afternoon. My father was standing in the front yard contemplating the crab apple tree. He must not have gone inside yet because his briefcase lay near him in the grass.

"This looks like it's dying," he said. He'd been wanting to cut down that tree for as far back as I could remember. Whenever he had to mow the lawn, he'd feel like he first had to collect all the little hard apples that had fallen so that they wouldn't break the blades.

"Looks fine to me," I said.

"I'm not so sure. The leaves don't seem to be turning, they're just dropping."

I picked up a couple of the apples to juggle them.

"You look happy," he said.

"There's just this guy at school I like and now I think he might like me."

"Well," he said, pressing his hand against the trunk. "Don't go and lose your head."

"God, Daddy, you're sounding like Mom."

"What do you think?" he asked, looking up through the branches. "Do you think it's dying?"

"I don't know anything about trees."

"No," he sighed, brushing the bark off his hands. He reached for his briefcase. "I guess I don't either."

"I HOPE THIS isn't too pink," said Deirdre, opening a lipstick she'd just bought. We'd stopped to sit on a bench at the mall, having spent almost an hour in the drugstore while she smeared different shades of lipstick onto the back of her hand. "You know, the more I think about it, the more I think you and Todd would make a good couple," she said.

I hadn't told her about what had happened with Todd, afraid that talking about it might somehow jinx my chances with him. "You do?"

"Why do you sound surprised?"

"We're so different," I said. "I mean, he's so creative and I'm not."

"Opposites attract, remember? Maybe he can fill that side of you that you didn't know you had." Her pocket mirror lit up when she opened it, casting a white circle on her mouth. "Too pink?" she asked.

"Depends what you wear it with."

"In other words, too pink."

"Don't be paranoid, it's not too pink." We were sitting in front of the artificial pond shaped like a heart. The underwater lights that rimmed the edge had long since burned out, so that the pennies at the bottom were blackened into a tarlike mass. "Do you think they're sleeping together?" I asked.

"Probably," she said. "They've been together long enough."

I stared out at the crowds of people passing by us and found myself looking for him, even though I'd never before seen him at the mall. But I was always looking for him now, always hoping that he'd suddenly appear. That he'd appear alone, without Caroline. "It's just weird to think about it."

"Sex is no big deal really, anyway."

I looked at her. "You're the one who's always saying how you're waiting around for just the right guy."

"I am. But . . . well, I'm not exactly a virgin anymore."

"You're not? When did *this* happen?"

"This summer. At my uncle's ranch in Montana. My cousin was there and we just somehow got together."

"Your *cousin?*"

"We're only distant cousins. And we went horseback riding one afternoon . . . anyway, it just sort of happened." She opened a can of soda, throwing the wrapper from her straw into the pot of a plastic tree beside the bench where there were other wrappers and old cigarettes. "It happened so quickly. Much more quickly than I ever thought it could." She shrugged. "So it just didn't seem to count."

Sex with Chip had almost "just sort of happened," but I was sure that if I ever slept with Todd it wouldn't be like that. We'd take our time and I'd feel like I could feel when I only had to think of him—a rush of warmth sometimes so intense it left me breathless.

A mother handed her little boy a penny to throw into the pond. He stared long and hard into the water and I remembered when I used to stare like that into that same pond. "You think it could still be a big deal then?" I asked.

"I hope so," she said, sipping her soda. She gently

blew bubbles through her straw. "If it's with the right guy."

I HAD FINISHED painting the fireplace and was now working on a flat with some other students, so Todd and I couldn't be alone as we could before. I'd follow him into the storeroom where he'd set up his worktable, pretending I was looking for a fresh paint can, and we'd end up kissing in the far corner by the pile of scrap wood. But these meetings were always as if by accident, and whenever I looked at him he'd avoid my gaze, looking somewhere over my shoulder. "I can't believe you," he'd say, running his hands up and down my sides. "You've got the kind of body not even a camera could put pounds on." I told myself to be patient, that it was just a matter of time before he'd feel able to make a real choice between me and Caroline.

On the night of the party, I arrived early to help Deirdre get ready, but she was still up in her room getting dressed. She sat at her desk that she'd transformed into a vanity, having plugged in a large brightly lit mirror and surrounded herself with a variety of blushes and eye shadows.

She took one look at me and said, "You look like a ghost."

"Thanks a lot."

"You just need a little something more," she said,

sitting me down at her desk. "Mascara and lip gloss don't quite do it."

"You were the one who said I didn't need makeup."

"Anyone needs makeup at night—you want Todd to be able to *see* you," she said, smearing a bright pink on my cheeks.

"Deirdre, I'm going to look like a clown."

"Will you relax? Give me a chance to blend it."

"Todd's going to know I'm doing this for him."

"Isn't that the idea?" Deirdre laughed.

"I don't want him to think I'm trying to steal him away from Caroline."

"But you *are*. He'll be flattered. After all, you're a lot prettier than she is."

She told me to close my eyes so that she could apply some eye shadow, and I said a little prayer. I prayed he wouldn't show up with Caroline.

WHEN WE CAME downstairs, her parents were on their way out, to a formal dance at the country club. The first time I'd gone to the club had been as Deirdre's guest, to swim in the pool, and she'd made a point of telling me, "We're not rich, you know." We'd been standing in the club's lobby and I'd been gazing around at the enormous flower arrangements on the mahogany tables. "We just act like it."

I'd thought that only rich people belonged to country

clubs. But the more time I spent at Deirdre's house, the more clearly I began to see that their worn oriental rugs, the chipped Chinese vases and the old baby grand piano with the yellowed keys really were only hand-me-downs, inherited from Deirdre's great-grandmother. Her father was a salesman for Hallmark cards. Once her parents had left, we pushed aside the piano and rolled up the orientals to make room for dancing.

The place was already crowded even before Todd arrived, and I couldn't bear to think that he might not come at all. Someone had offered me a beer and I took it, even though I usually just drank Coke.

I was on my second beer when he finally showed up—with Caroline. All my hopes seemed to fizzle and I stayed against the wall talking with some friends. But I kept glancing over at him as they moved around the room.

Deirdre pulled me aside. "I can't believe it. Katie and all her little friends are in the kitchen watching TV."

"It's your house," I said. "If you don't want the TV on, go turn it off."

She began peeling the label off her beer bottle. "I can't."

"Why not?"

"Because I *can't*," she snapped. She made her way around the edges of the room placing coasters under all the beer and Coke cans people had left on the piano.

I looked back at Todd. They'd settled on the couch and Caroline was avidly talking to one of her girlfriends. While Todd listened patiently, he was fingering the shade of the Tiffany wall lamp above their heads. At one point he glanced up at the shade, and I knew he was admiring the stained glass; sometimes I'd see him like that backstage. He'd look so alone in his thoughtfulness as he paused to admire the grain in a piece of wood that I'd wish he could feel how I watched him.

As if he could feel me now, he looked in my direction. He noticed me for what seemed the first time that night. He took his hand down from the lamp and I thought he might actually get up and come over to me.

He looked away, avoiding my gaze as he would in the storeroom. He stretched out his arm along the back of the couch behind Caroline and whispered something to her. They got up and, taking her by the hand, he led her onto the dance floor. Even though it was a fast song, he held her close. They danced slowly. He looked into her face in a way he had never been able to look into mine, and I realized he'd finally made his choice—he'd chosen Caroline over me.

I saw myself then, but not as Chip would have seen me. I saw how alone I must have seemed, standing there peeling the label off my beer bottle. I had to leave. I ran upstairs to Deirdre's room where I'd left my coat.

The door was shut, and when I opened it Deirdre was sitting at her desk in front of her vanity mirror. She got up with a start, but when she saw that it was only me she sat back down. She'd been crying and her mascara had smeared so that she had large black smudges under her eyes.

"What's the matter?" I asked, not really wanting to know.

"Look at me!" She took the entire bridge out of her mouth and threw it across her desk. "See? This is what I really am. And Katie knows it. She can know it without even seeing it."

"You're really obsessed, Deirdre, you know that?"

"You can't tell me you don't wish you were like that, so adored. Think about it, how great it would feel to have everyone adoring you."

The only light in the room beyond the stark glow of her vanity mirror came from the street lamps. It fell through her venetian blinds in harsh yellow rows, and I needed to be outside

I grabbed my coat. "You can't leave me," I heard her calling as I ran down the stairs.

IT WAS GREAT to be out in the air, the music now reduced to a bass sound. I walked home, not caring that my father was waiting up for me to call so he could drive me. I cut through people's backyards and even climbed over a wire mesh fence, and I realized I must have been kind of drunk.

I accidentally kicked over one of my mother's flowerpots on the front step, and I waited for my father to appear at the door. I went inside and found him asleep in front of the television. He looked old and tired with his head back and his mouth open, and he reminded me of my grandfather again. "Daddy!" I called sharply.

He sat up with a start. "How'd you get home?"

"I walked."

"You *walked*? Leslie, that's crazy. You know I don't like you doing that at night, anything could happen."

"Nothing did happen, did it?"

He examined me. "Are you all right?"

"I'm great. I'm just fine."

"Well," he said, sitting back. "We won't tell your mother about this. You know how she'd feel." He picked up a book, a large old bound one of Blake that I recognized from his shelf. "Go on up to bed."

I went upstairs, relieved that he'd been unable to see that I'd been drinking; before he'd become so distracted, he'd been able to tell when I'd had even a single glass of wine.

I WOKE UP around noon and lay in bed for a long time, staring over at my window seat where I kept all my old dolls. Long neglected, they lay this way and that, their limbs twisted, and I wondered if that wasn't how people looked when they died. My head was pounding and I decided that this must be my first hangover.

I heard my mother outside. She sounded so upset I ran downstairs in only my nightgown. She and my father were standing over by the crab apple tree.

"Please, Dale, please," she cried. "That tree's been there forever."

"It's dead, Marion, look at it," said my father, untangling the cord to his electric saw. I never thought he would actually cut it down; some of my mother's favorite birds nested in there every spring and that had been enough reason for him not to.

"There must be some way to save it," I said, less because I cared about the tree than because I was alarmed by how oblivious he seemed to my mother's feelings.

"Look at it!" he yelled, turning on the saw.

Above its piercing wail I could no longer hear my mother's pleading. She pulled on his shirt, but as the saw actually began cutting into the trunk she backed away. She turned and ran inside.

I too wanted to run away. At the same time I wanted to see the tree fall. I had thought, hoped, it would fall with a great crash. It fell quietly, cushioned by its branches. It took up almost the entire lawn, and my father stood there rubbing his chin and staring at what he had done.

I thought of Todd, but not in the way I used to, in the way I wanted to, when the thought of him could surround me in a warm haze. Now the thought of him left me feeling so ugly and foolish I could barely stand myself, and I cried out, "What is it, Daddy? What's happening? What's happening to us?"

He sat down on the stump. He began to cry. I'd never seen him cry before. "My God," he said, running his hand through his hair. "Your mother loved that tree."

My mother. I looked toward the house. She was staring out from the large picture window that had always been shaded by that tree. Against the clouds now reflected there, she was a mirage. I couldn't quite see her.

EIGHT

I would always remember that day. How it had been so sunny, so warm for October, but, watching my father cry, I had felt as if I could never really be outside again, not in the way I could when I'd still known how to feel the open spaces of the beach, of Indian Lake, even of our own front yard.

He moved out the following March. He would have left sooner if I hadn't begged him to stay. One rainy afternoon he came into my room and sat on my bed, saying, "Leslie, I just can't do it anymore." I sat at my desk penciling thick rings around the holes in my spiral-bound notebook. He kept his head bowed. "I just can't."

I allowed him to leave my room then as easily as if he had been helping me with math problems. I never thought he'd actually move out.

He left hardly anything behind, in his study a few old critical texts from his classes in Romantic poetry and Shakespeare, texts he now considered to be outdated. He left his globe which was also a lamp. He wanted me to have it but I told him I didn't care about having the globe, didn't care about him leaving behind anything at all. He left the globe anyway, to stand alone on his study floor. He must have known I would be unable to resist spreading my hands across those mountains in relief, closing my eyes to concentrate on their gravelly feel.

What he hadn't stayed around long enough to see was that there were little green shoots now growing out of the stump of the crab apple tree; it hadn't been dead after all.

THREE WEEKS LATER, at two in the morning I looked out my window and saw my mother standing in the light of the open cellar door. Her bathrobe hung open, revealing the peach satin nightgown my father had given her one anniversary. She held a small wooden chair upside down as she examined its legs. Scattered across the driveway were more chairs and a drop-leaf table, things she had collected over the years from garage sales and had intended to refinish. She put the chair down and it toppled over. One leg was broken. Hugging herself, she turned and disappeared down the steps.

I went down to the cellar. She was standing under the bare bulb dangling from the ceiling examining what looked like a giant brandy snifter. She'd tied back her hair into a bristly ponytail with a piece of yarn she must have found down there.

"Oh, did I wake you?" she asked. "This cellar just hasn't been cleaned out since I don't know when." She balanced the bowl on her palm, her face distorted behind it so that her eyes grew round as marbles. "Isn't this lovely? It's a terrarium and I'd forgotten all about it. Once I grew wild berries in it, I think."

I sat on the stairs. The walls were blank except for an old kitchen cabinet filled with chipped china, half-melted candles, broken cameras given away by banks, all those things that weren't quite useless but for which there was no real place.

I STILL SOMETIMES thought about Todd, although I tried not to. After Deirdre's party we'd met only once more in the storeroom but didn't end up kissing over by the pile of scrap wood again. I'd gone in there for a clean brush and he was standing over his worktable, a piece of plywood stretched across two sawhorses. He stiffened when he saw me, slipping one hand into his tool belt.

"You don't have to avoid me," I'd said.

"I'm not avoiding you," he said uneasily.

"You were at the party."

He took out a nail and examined it. "I guess I felt funny. Me and Caroline, well . . . I started worrying about that."

"What is it about her?"

"Caroline?"

"Do you love her?"

"I guess I do." He shrugged. "I really trust her."

I leaned back against the door. "What went on with us wasn't anything."

"I thought you liked it. I mean, you did start it . . ." Then he asked incredulously, "Did you think me and Caroline would break up or something?"

I realized more fully than I had even at the party just how much more I'd been thinking about him than he'd ever been thinking about me. "Let's just forget all this, okay?" I said, looking down at the floor and drawing an arc in the sawdust with my foot.

"Sure," he said, sounding very relieved. He began hammering, as if I'd already left the room.

I SPOTTED A spider web up in one corner wavering slightly, precariously, and felt the emptiness of the house above us. "It smells gross down here," I said.

"You wouldn't believe the junk," said my mother, setting the terrarium on top of the laundry machine. "And what am I going to do with all these?" She slapped her hand on top of a bookshelf full of *National Geographics*. "Your father has been saving them since before you were born, and I don't think he's looked at them since."

I got off the steps to thumb through an issue. An

article had been cut out and replaced by a perfect L-shaped hole, probably an article having to do with anthropology, something that had always interested my father. I saw him suddenly, sitting on the living room window seat where he had enjoyed reading in the natural light, carefully clipping out the article with the tiny scissors from his pocketknife. "I'll use them," I said, flipping closed the magazine. "For school projects."

"That was always your father's excuse too," said my mother, pulling out the magazines and stacking them on the floor. "The point is, he's gone and left them here for me to get rid of."

She crouched to open a battered cardboard box tucked next to the bookshelf. "Now why do you suppose he saved these?" she said, taking out an empty wire spool and a handle that must have belonged to a hammer. "There's not one worthwhile object in here and all of it belongs to your father."

I stood over her where I could see down her nightgown to her breasts that were no bigger than mine. This pleased me immensely. "You're the one who's always going around to all those garage sales and picking up beat-up old furniture."

A needle-straight strand of my mother's hair hung over one eye. "You're right. Absolutely right. And I'm throwing all that furniture out. Everything." She emptied the box into a garbage bag, its contents knocking noisily against what sounded like broken glass. "I'd like to just throw out every single thing."

I watched the heels of her slippers flap up the stone steps to the driveway. When she came back down, I said, "Maybe he'll change his mind."

She stopped in front of me. Her eyes narrowed into slits.

"Maybe he'll come home," I said.

She leaned on the laundry machine. "Maybe," she said, flicking her finger so gently against the rim of the terrarium the glass barely chimed. "You should go see him." She sighed. "At least talk to him when he calls."

I examined a nail. "Why?"

"Because." She picked up a ball of blue lint near the dryer and squeezed it between two fingers. "I'm tired of his calling."

For something to do, more than out of curiosity, I lifted the lid of a trunk next to the hot-water heater. Inside were neatly folded scraps of material which I recognized from all our old slipcovers and curtains. As much as I couldn't blame him for leaving, I couldn't help feeling angry. I pressed my hands into their bright patterns. "I don't want to see him."

"You want to see him more than you can stand."

I shut the trunk. "I think I'll go back to bed."

"Wait," she said, taking hold of my arm. "Since you're up, why don't you help me a little?"

"Is the world really going to end if you don't get this done by dawn?"

"If you could do one thing," she said, smoothing out the tiny bow at the neckline of her nightgown. "If you could just help me take out the lounge chairs. We'll be wanting to use them before long. Then I promise not to bother you about it anymore. I promise."

THE SLATE OF the patio was colder than the cement floor of the cellar, and after we'd set up the chairs I sat on the edge of one to rub my feet.

My mother stretched out on the other chair and looked at the sky. "Almost a full moon, just one slice missing." She dangled her arms over the back of the chair and wiggled her toes. "It's going to be a blue moon next month. Two full moons in one month. Imagine that." She looked at me and, smiling, said, "Wouldn't that be wonderful if the moon really *were* blue?"

My father would have loved her at this moment, the way one corner of her mouth was lifted half shyly, half playfully. But he wasn't here. I was angry with her for wasting her charm on me.

My mother seemed disappointed when I didn't answer. She looked back at the sky. "You remember how you used to run off when you were little?" she asked. "You would wander off within a matter of seconds and a neighbor down the street, or a few times it was the owner of the cleaners, would call and ask if you were our daughter. I was thinking about that. You know, when I'm up like this. And I was wondering if you'd ever had a destination in mind." She looked at me again. The moon painted her as white as the lawn, as the trunks of the maple trees. "Did you?"

"I wasn't running away, Mom."

She laughed, tightening her ponytail. "Of course not."

I started to get up.

"It's so nice out here, don't you want to sit a few more minutes?" she asked.

"I'm kind of cold. It's not exactly summer."

"Oh, don't be so warm-blooded."

"Good night, Mom."

"Leslie?"

I stopped without turning around.

"We'll be all right, you know."

I stared at three empty flowerpots piled one within the other on the edge of the patio. They appeared about to fall over, but they had stood crookedly like that all winter. "Yeah."

I kept walking. Behind me I heard my mother whispering softly to herself, "Yes, yes, we'll be all right."

IN THE MORNING, I was already dressed and eating a bowl of Cheerios when my mother came into the kitchen.

She appeared stooped in a lavender dress whose shoulder pads fell forward.

"Did you finish?" I asked.

"The cellar's spick-and-span. We could live down there." She gazed out the window above the sink as she filled the kettle. "The garden's next, I suppose. It's almost the end of April and I haven't even turned over the ground." She sat opposite me and trickled cereal into a bowl. "It would be nice, don't you think? If just for once morning didn't have to come. If we didn't have to get up and do everything all over again."

The cereal sat in her bowl. I waited for her to get up for the milk in the refrigerator. Instead, she tried to fix her shoulder pads.

"I thought we might do something together tonight," she said. "It's Friday."

I scraped the bottom of my bowl with my spoon. "I'm going to the movies."

"Oh," she said, glancing down at her front, brushing it as if she'd spilled something.

I couldn't stand how hurt she looked and I got up to drop my dishes into the sink. "I've got to get going."

"You're always rushing off so."

"I've got school, Mom," I said, quickly gathering up my books from the counter and swinging my purse over my shoulder. I kissed her briefly.

"You know if your father were home you wouldn't

be going off doing whatever it is you want. You know that, don't you?"

I left through the kitchen door.

A moment later her voice splintered the morning quiet. "Don't you!"

I walked quickly down the driveway, my purse knocking painfully against my hips.

IT WAS ALREADY late when Deirdre and I and a friend of ours, Judy, got out of the movies. But I didn't want to go home. I didn't want to have to see my mother, who was probably still up, cleaning again. "Let's drive around for a little," I said.

"I promised I'd get the car right back," said Deirdre. She'd only had her license a month, but she was among the first of my friends to get one.

"We don't have to go far, just down Plank Road or something."

"*Plank Road?*" Judy exclaimed. "There's nothing down Plank Road. And it's awfully dark to be just riding around."

I wished Judy wasn't with us. I was tired of her always taking Deirdre's side. She couldn't buy a single pair of shoes or a new shade of blush without first consulting Deirdre.

"That's the *idea*," I said. "There wouldn't be any cars. And it's only a couple of blocks from here." I looked over at Deirdre who stood on the other side of the car. "Let's not go home yet," I nearly pleaded.

Even in the dim lights of the parking lot I could see how Deirdre was worrying, loosening her bridge so that it looked as if she was sucking on a large piece of candy. She wouldn't think to actually flick her teeth out in front of Judy, who would have been crushed to find out that Deirdre wasn't perfect. Deirdre claimed not to care anymore about Katie, even though at parties she'd still gaze longingly at her.

"Well," said Deirdre, spinning her keys on the car hood, "I guess it would be kind of fun to just cruise."

Plank Road was exactly like that, a plank. It stretched straight and narrow between two fields. The land had been leveled off there some years ago for a shopping complex that was never built. Nothing was there now except for patches of weeds and some abandoned tires.

"You're driving like a little old lady," I said.

"I can't help it," said Deirdre. "Look at this fog. It wasn't this foggy out on the main road."

"Turn off your brights," I said. "You're not supposed to use brights in fog. They make it worse."

"I never learned that in driver's ed. Where'd you hear that?"

"My father. He takes me out sometimes." I turned up the radio.

"Please don't," said Deirdre. "I have to concentrate."

"It's not like you're on a freeway," I laughed.

"She's only had her license a month," Judy chimed in.

"Yeah," said Deirdre, "wait until you get your license and you're driving your parents' car, you'll see."

"I can't wait," I said, looking out across the fields. I could see the lights of the mall where we'd been for the movie, and it was like looking out at a distant city. "I'd be halfway across the country by now."

"That *would* be cool," said Deirdre. "To drive cross-country. I'd head straight for the Blue Ridge Mountains."

"I'd go to Florida," said Judy.

"Florida's boring. People go there to die."

"What about the Everglades?" asked Judy, sounding wounded.

"I once drove across Arizona with my parents," said Deirdre, "and it was just like this—one long road. Except it went on for miles and miles. You could go seventy and feel like you were still only going fifty."

"Go seventy," I said.

"No way."

"Come on, just for a minute. At least go sixty. You're not even going that."

"Well . . ." said Deirdre, already stepping on the gas. "Maybe sixty."

I opened my window so that I could feel the speed.

"Oh, I love this song," said Deirdre, turning up the radio herself this time.

The night seemed to be at our mercy until suddenly she was slamming on the brakes.

In the next moment the car was off the road and there was the sound of branches scraping across the hood. The headlights shone into a cluster of trees. Deirdre had driven straight up onto an island where the road forked off.

We sat there in a stunned silence until Deirdre stammered, "I didn't see it, I didn't see the fork . . ."

"It's the fog," came Judy's voice, shakily, from the backseat.

"No," said Deirdre. "I was going too fast. I shouldn't have been going so fast—"

"We didn't hit anything," I said weakly.

"We could have, Leslie!" she yelled at me, suddenly hysterical. "We could have smashed up my parents' car!"

I stared at the fog falling through the headlights.

"Let's just get back," said Judy, her voice sounding smaller and smaller.

Deirdre backed carefully off the island. She drove home very slowly. She'd turned off the radio, so that the only sound was an occasional piece of gravel knocking against a hubcap. We didn't talk at all. Our silence now seemed less stunned than embarrassed, as if our dreams about driving across the country had been purely childish.

———

WHEN I GOT home, my mother was polishing the andirons in the living room.

"Do you know what time it is?" she asked, confronting me in the hall.

"It's not that late," I mumbled.

She rubbed her palm across the quilted rabbit on her apron. A carrot was stitched to the pocket. She'd made the apron herself back when sewing had been her interest. "We can't go on like this," she said.

I started up the stairs.

She grabbed the back of my shirt. "*Talk* to me, please."

"About what? What is it you want to talk about?"

"Anything. Tell me anything."

"All right—we almost crashed tonight."

"*Crashed?*"

"We almost got killed, in fact. And where would you be now? How could you *possibly* survive!" I yelled.

She let go of me, backing down the stairs. She sat on the bottom step, leaning back against the railing as if suddenly exhausted. It was a long time before she said anything. When she did, she gazed up at me, and I saw what dark shadows she had under her eyes. "Maybe you should stay with your father for a while. Maybe we . . . maybe you and I need time apart."

The rabbit's ears were frayed. The apron was old, but I could remember her sewing it. I could remember admiring the quick rhythm of her needle. "Mom . . . I don't know." I came down and sat next to her on the step. I'd thought about that, living with my father, but I'd never thought that she'd actually suggest it herself.

She smiled thinly. "I've loved you too much, haven't I?"

"Yeah. Maybe."

She only nodded, and something felt different between us. Maybe it was the way we both sat there with our knees drawn up; sometimes I'd sit like that on the front stoop with one of my friends. As if we were just passing time together.

But then she got up. "Call him," she said, slowly climbing the stairs, leaning heavily on her thighs. "Call him tomorrow."

THE NEXT MORNING I did call my father, after watching my mother for a long time out the kitchen window. She was pitchforking her garden and wore an old wide-brimmed Easter bonnet as a sun hat. I didn't know whether we really needed time apart, that I would be any happier at my father's new apartment. I only knew that I missed him terribly. I called him from the den.

I was unprepared for how nervous I felt when he picked up the phone. "Daddy?"

He sighed. "Leslie. I knew you'd come around. I've missed you."

I settled myself on the couch, bringing up my knees to my chin. "Daddy."

"This will all take time," he said. It sounded as if he had turned on a faucet. "Just remember that."

The sound of running water grew louder. "Are you in your kitchen?" I asked.

"Catching up on a few dishes."

"I can't imagine what it looks like. Your kitchen. I keep seeing ours."

"It's not like ours at all."

"What color is it?"

"Mostly blue."

Ours was wallpapered with yellow daisies.

"Daddy, Mom thinks maybe I should come stay with you for a while."

"Honey." He turned off the faucet. "I don't know about that."

I sat up on the edge of the couch and twisted the phone cord around my wrist.

"There really isn't room here. I mean, I have a room for you, but . . . I need time to myself, honey. I need time to get myself on my feet. I need that space. Can you understand that?"

"I won't get in your way."

"That's not the point. It just can't happen, not now."

"When?"

He sighed and there was a long pause. "Leslie, I've

been . . . seeing someone. It's nothing serious, more for companionship than anything else. Please don't tell your mother, that's all she needs to hear right now."

I stared at the rug, at the interlocking cream-colored circles that began to pulsate.

He cleared his throat. "It's nothing to upset yourself about, really. The point is, it wouldn't be comfortable here for you."

I leaned my forehead against the wall. All I could see were the knots in the paneling.

"I love you, Leslie, you know that."

I shut my eyes.

"Will you come see me soon? How about next weekend? You can give me some decorating tips on this place. How about that?"

"I don't know."

"Please say yes."

"Yes," I echoed.

"Great." The water was turned on again. "I'll call you during the week to set up a time. I love you."

"Yes, Daddy." I hung up the phone.

I gazed down at my feet planted on the floor. They seemed to grow, to become bloated as if submerged underwater. I felt that not even Chip would want to touch me now. It was a long time before I moved from the couch. When I did get up, the only thing I could think of to do was go outside and find my mother.

———

SHE KNELT IN front of her garden bed digging small holes with a trowel and sprinkling peat moss and fertilizer into them. The petals of the large pink and yellow paper roses on her hat flapped in a breeze. She leaned back on her heels, smiling thinly at me as she had last night. "Isn't it absolutely a perfect day?" She pointed toward the edge of the yard. "And look who has been watching me."

Our neighbors' four-year-old child, Rosey Williams, crouched on the other side of the hedge. She clutched a doll by the hair.

"It's nice to think I could be so fascinating," said my mother, waving at her. Rosey looked down shyly, twisting the arm of her doll full circle. The other arm was missing.

I sat cross-legged next to my mother. "I called Daddy."

My mother tipped her hat down. Shadows flooded her face. She popped a pink flower from a cubicle in a plastic tray and lowered it carefully into one of the holes. "Oh? And what did he have to say?"

I split a blade of grass down the middle. "Something about needing space."

"Space?" She stabbed her trowel into the ground. "He's got the best of both worlds now, don't you see? He's got his precious freedom."

Rosey shifted. Her sneakers squeaked against the pavement of their driveway.

"Oh, who knows," my mother sighed, letting go of her trowel and leaning back on her arms. She closed her eyes against the sun. "Maybe he'll come back still. And what would we do then, you and I, if he came crawling back?"

"He won't."

She looked at me hopefully. "But you said so yourself. And maybe that's what he meant by space—he needs time to think."

"He's not coming back."

"You don't know. He could actually be missing us—"

"He's seeing someone, Mom."

She stared blindly at her garden, at the holes she had dug but not yet filled.

"I didn't mean to tell you. He told me not to tell you, I don't know why I did . . ."

Slowly she raised her eyes and looked at Rosey. "I bet you'd like to come over and play, wouldn't you? I know. I'll be right back." She tore off her garden gloves and ran lightly across the yard to the house. I stared at her gloves, so stiff with dirt they were sculptures in the grass.

My mother returned with a bag of chocolate chip cookies. She held it out toward the hedge. "Don't these look good, Rosey?"

, Rosey dropped her doll and squeezed through the hedge. She appeared in our yard, scratching her elbows. Her Big Bird T-shirt didn't quite cover her stomach and a full head of kinky curls framed her round face.

"Aren't you a butterball," said my mother, handing Rosey a cookie and taking her into her lap. Rosey's eyes grew glassy as she concentrated on the cookie. My mother held another cookie poised in the air which she gave her as soon as Rosey had finished the first one.

"I'm not so sure Mrs. Williams would appreciate your feeding her like that," I said.

My mother ignored me.

Finally Rosey seemed full, puckering her lips irritably against another cookie. She began to squirm. "Oh, you don't have to go yet," my mother cooed. "Here, look." She took off her Easter hat. Rosey plucked furiously at the flowers.

The Williams's door slammed. "Rosey? Rosey!"

"Mom, you should let her go."

"She's all right," my mother whispered. She rocked back and forth, pressing Rosey's face against her chest so that her whimpering was stifled. "She's fine, just fine," sang my mother. Mrs. Williams's large form in a lime green dress flashed behind the hedge as she searched their yard. The more she called, the harder my mother rocked.

I knew I should get up and pry Rosey loose. But our survival from this moment to the next seemed to depend on her not getting away. I prayed that Mrs. Williams wouldn't hear her daughter. I prayed that Rosey would quiet down so that my mother could cradle her peacefully.

Rosey punched my mother in the lower part of her abdomen, just missing her crotch. As my mother doubled over in pain, she lost her grip and Rosey, screaming, ran free. She fell once, picked herself up quickly and scrambled through the bushes.

Mrs. Williams scooped her up, peered briefly at us through the hedge, then disappeared inside their house. Rosey's cries were severed by the slam of their door. The doll gleamed where it lay on the other side of the hedge, half naked.

"She could be a pretty little girl," said my mother, rubbing her abdomen.

"Yes, she could be," I said, believing in this more fully than I had believed in anything for a long time.

My mother looked down at her hat. It lay crumpled in her lap, the paper flowers dangling by threads. I put it on my own head so she would have to look at me. That made her laugh.

NINE

My father picked me up the following Saturday morning. I had intended to slide into his old Mustang, lifting my wedge-heeled shoes and pulling up my jeans at the knees, but instead dropped clumsily into the bucket seat. My father had come around to my side. He shut my door and peered at me through my open window.

"Don't you look pretty," he said.

"Yeah," I said, trying not to sound pleased.

In the pocket of his favorite spring sports jacket were clipped the usual red pen and refillable pencil. I wanted to run my fingers along the pocket, pull off the caps and click the lead from the pencil, the way I used to. But I was seeing him only for the day, I would be coming home without him. I closed my fist around the window handle.

Gently he flicked one of my dangling silver earrings. "You finally got your ears pierced." He took my chin in his hand. "And a little more makeup too, huh?"

Turning my face away, I pulled myself up so I could see the metallic horse on the hood. "Anything else?"

He walked around the front of the car and got in beside me. "Just surprised your mother's letting you wear eye shadow."

"She's not stopping me."

He laughed. "So that's it. Just like her."

"Just like what?"

"Unable to say no to you."

My mother had planted pansies along the brick walk as she did every year. The faces I saw in their petals were both tortured and laughing and then not faces at all. I'd begun to see faces inside the house as well, in the perforated pattern of the dining room lamp shades when my mother and I sat opposite each other at dinner.

As we backed out of the driveway I raised my eyes to her bedroom window where the shades were still drawn. She'd gone back to bed after breakfast, not wanting to be around when my father picked me up. She probably had a damp washcloth draped across her eyes and the fake ocean crashing rhythmically from the sound box she had bought to calm her nerves.

"I'm glad you finally decided to see me," said my father.

Without looking, I knew his arm was outstretched to catch the breezes in his open palm. "Mom insisted."

"Well, I like to think you wanted to see me just a little bit."

"Why should I?"

He withdrew his arm from the window and gripped the wheel with both hands. "Someday soon, Leslie, I hope you will be able to accept all this."

"You're already seeing someone."

"I told you, it's nothing serious."

I opened my purse, a sequined satchel that hung past my hips, and took out a stick of Juicy Fruit. My father hated my chewing gum, not because of the sugar but because he thought it was "common." I folded it into my mouth. "So what are we going to do?"

"First, a few errands."

I snapped my gum. "What fun."

WE STOPPED AT the bank. "I'll be right back," he said, slamming the door, shutting me into the silence. He was whisked out of the sun by the closing glass door as if I'd dreamt him.

The clock ticked madly in the dashboard. I shifted

to peel my jeans away from the vinyl. They were too tight in the crotch. Sweat dripped from my armpits, even though it wasn't hot. I breathed deeply, leaned my head back and closed my eyes so that I could lose myself in the sun bursting behind my lids. I didn't open my eyes until my father got back into the car.

"Next are groceries," he said.

"Can I drive?"

He looked at me as if he didn't understand.

"I *can* drive, you know. You taught me, remember?"

He turned the key in the ignition. "Maybe later."

AT THE A&P my father gazed from one shelf to another as I had seen him gaze at paintings when we strolled through museums together.

"What are you looking for anyway?" I asked, pushing the cart.

"The essentials, I guess." He paused in front of the rice shelf. "It would be so much easier if they just had one of everything, not all these different brands." He dropped a box of Uncle Ben's into the cart. "At least that's basic. No fancy gravies or beef flavors. Can't go wrong there."

I glided on one foot, leaning heavily on the cart. "Do you order out a lot?"

"I guess I do."

"Pizza?"

"Sometimes. Usually Chinese food."

"Mom would faint if she knew you were eating pizza."

He nodded, squeezing a loaf of Wonder Bread. "She would, wouldn't she?" He helped me push the cart with one hand, the other deep in his pocket jingling change. "How is she anyway? You can't tell much over the phone."

"She's up a lot at night, cleaning."

"Cleaning?"

"The other night I woke up and she was cleaning out the cellar."

My father let go of the cart to put his other hand in his pocket.

"You're worried about her," I said.

"Well, don't sound so surprised."

I gathered my silver spangles into a row on my wrist. "Who is this other woman anyway?"

He laughed. "She's not exactly the 'other woman.' She's just someone new teaching in the anthropology department."

"Do you really like her?"

"She's a nice lady and we enjoy each other's company." We'd stopped in front of the frozen-food section. He balanced a bag of string beans on his palm. "It's hard not to feel like I'm cheating on your mother."

We got in line. The frozen vegetables, Wonder

Bread, all those items my mother would never buy, rolled down the conveyor belt as if they were for someone else. My father pulled out crumpled bills and straightened them. I used to watch him clean fish, then carefully cut out for me the eye lenses, round and clear as tiny crystal balls. His hands still seemed miraculously strong and nimble.

"You want to drive now?" he asked, as we carried the bags out to the car.

"That's okay."

"You can if you want to. We can take the small side streets back to my apartment."

"Thanks. But I like the way you drive just fine."

"Well, I'm deeply flattered." He opened the car door for me. "Really."

"Who lives downstairs?" I asked, as we stood on his front porch. He was fishing through his pockets for the single key he hadn't yet put on his key chain. White petunias in macramé hangers framed his neighbor's door. Outside his own there was only a green welcome mat.

"A nice older couple. She's great, treats me like her son, always making me brownies."

I looked around the living room while my father carried the groceries into the kitchen. The large oak desk from his study was squeezed between one wall and his two towering filing cabinets. I picked up one of the English papers strewn across the floor and recognized my father's scrawl in the margin. He had bracketed a paragraph and written, "Unclear." I put the paper back as I found it, half concealed by his grading notebook. The faded red couch from our den was against one wall—my mother was going to sell it anyway. Two end tables from our attic were lined up next to each other as if my father hadn't decided where to put them.

He came in and handed me a glass of ginger ale. "Sorry about this," he said, getting down on the floor and sweeping together the papers. "I'm right in the middle of finals."

I sat on the couch, fingering a familiar stain of spilled milk in the cushion. A maple blocked out most of the light from the two windows and I couldn't tell whether the walls were white or gray. The room was bathed in the cool darkness of a library and smelled like melted candles. My father, now on all fours, had taken off his jacket. One shirttail hung out. From where I sat I could see that the hair on the back of his head had begun to thin.

"So what do you think?" he asked.

"It's depressing."

"What did you expect, a fancy condominium?"

"Something more than this, Daddy. I thought you might have fixed it up a little."

"And I thought you might help me with that."

The papier-mâché dish I had made for him in kindergarten sat on his desk. I got up to look at it. It still held his paper clips. The edges were frayed and a piece broke off and crumbled easily. "Are you really happier living here?"

"Happier, I don't know. Saner, yes." He piled the last of the papers on his desk. "You'll find out one day happiness isn't everything."

"Great."

He tucked in his shirttail. "Would you like to see your room?"

"My room?"

"It has a balcony."

THE BALCONY WAS warped and too narrow for even folding chairs but it looked out on a cherry blossom tree. My father had bought for me the four glass shelves I'd asked for at Christmas, that my mother wouldn't buy because she was afraid they would shatter. They were circular, held together by a single slender brass pole in the middle and stacked like the layers of a wedding cake. I imagined now, as I had imagined when we all first saw them together at the mall, how I would arrange my jewelry box and collection of ceramic unicorns. I hadn't imagined the shelves in any other room besides my bedroom at home where they would have gone perfectly with my gold shag rug.

"I hope you still like them," my father said, from where he stood in the doorway.

I sat on the bed. "Thank you, Daddy." The only other furniture was a pine dresser with an unframed mirror hanging above it.

He saw me looking at it and said, "I bought that from the woman who lived here before."

"It's nice."

"We can paint the room a color if you want. It doesn't have to be white."

"Daddy? What's her name?"

"You don't need to know her name."

"I know I don't. But I want to know."

"Clarkson."

"Clarkson? That's her last name?"

"Her first. The maiden name of some great-aunt or something, I'm not sure." He sat beside me. "I wish this could be easier for you."

The shelves stood next to the bed. I pressed my fingers on the glass to watch my prints disappear.

"Tell me what I can do or say to make all this easier," he said.

"Tell me you don't love my mother anymore."

He gripped the edge of the bare mattress. "I can't tell you that."

"Then tell me you don't love me anymore."

"Leslie."

I got up to look in the mirror. The oil had already

surfaced through the powder around my nose and my lips had lost their sheen. "Then there's nothing you can do."

"Well then," said my father crisply, drumming his fingers on his knees, "why don't we put away the groceries?"

"In a minute."

He left me alone in the room. I emptied my purse on the bureau, scattering loose sticks of gum and eye pencils. I looked anxiously for my compact and lip gloss.

MY FATHER HELD the refrigerator open with his foot as he filled the egg tray in the door. "How's school going, anyway?"

"The usual."

"Your mother told me you got an eighty-five on your last math exam. You used to not be able to wait to tell me those things."

"You haven't been around to tell," I said, sitting down at his kitchen table.

He examined an egg as if looking for cracks. "She also told me you've been staying out pretty late."

"Thanks, Mom," I mumbled, rolling my eyes.

He sat opposite me. "You know, if I were home, you wouldn't be allowed to do that."

"You're not home."

"You don't need to turn everything around and make

it my fault. I just don't want to see you upset your mother. She's upset as it is."

"I'm not, Daddy."

He rotated the lid on the sugar bowl. "Subject closed. I've made my point. So now the day is ours. What would you like to do?"

I shrugged, taking out another stick of gum. I folded the old piece into the yellow wrapper and I saved the silver one to smooth out into a mirror with my nail.

"Do you have to chew that?"

I looked at him squarely. "Yes."

The sound of a skateboard on the sidewalk echoed obtrusively through the kitchen.

"You know, none of this is easy for me either," said my father, tilting back his chair. "I wonder if you've thought about that."

"Well, you're a free man now, aren't you?"

His chair legs snapped sharply against the floor as he leaned toward me. "I've had about enough of your short sassy remarks. And you can just spit out that gum or leave."

"Leave?"

"Yes, you're such a big girl now, you can take the bus."

"Daddy . . ."

"And don't turn on the tears. Because so far today I've been doing my best, while you're not trying at all."

Slowly I took the gum out of my mouth and rolled it into the wrapper.

"Thank you."

I stared across the linoleum floor.

"It hasn't been all fun and games for me either, Leslie—"

"Then why don't you just come home?" I said.

"Oh, Leslie."

"You still can. You know Mom wants you back. And you said you don't really care about this Clarkson woman."

He held his hands clasped behind his neck as he stared down at the table.

"You won't have to worry about me, I promise, I won't stay out late, I'll come home when you want me to—"

"Leslie, I *can't*."

A hope I hadn't even known was there collapsed inside me.

"What you don't understand is, I need to be on my own. After all these years, there are things I want to do . . ." He opened the sugar bowl and sprinkled a little onto the table. "I'm getting older, Leslie."

He continued to pile the sugar crystals until he had formed a pyramid, and he seemed suddenly boyish to me. Like all those boys in school who couldn't concentrate for very long, who would make little piles of confetti on their desks. I could no longer look at him and I got up. I walked over to the counter and stared at the blue tiles lining the wall above the sink and beneath the cabinets. A young girl picked flowers outside a windmill and sheep grazed. I saw they weren't real tiles at all, only pictures reproduced on contact paper. "It's not just Mom then."

I wanted him to reassure me that his leaving was indeed because of my mother, that it was still that simple. I didn't want to know that it was so much more; that even if things had been better between my parents, possibly it wouldn't have mattered. I didn't want to know what now seemed to be the truth—my mother and I just no longer were enough.

He didn't say anything.

I faced him. "Where do you get off, just throwing it all away?"

"I'm not throwing it all away."

"Then what do you call it?"

He didn't answer me.

I leaned on the table in front of him. "Didn't you tell me happiness isn't everything?"

He just looked at me.

"*Didn't* you?"

"My God," he said quietly, shaking his head, "how I'm hurting you."

I had to look away, surprised at how suddenly his

face came undone by an expression close to horror. I looked down at the floor where I saw that one of his shoes was untied. I didn't think as I crouched to tie the laces into a strong bow, and I leaned against his knee. I started to cry then, not really knowing that I was going to cry.

"Leslie . . ." he barely whispered. He stroked my hair. "I'm so sorry."

I felt as if I'd been thrown there, as if I'd never be able to get up off that floor. I cried as I hadn't since he left, heaving, pressing my hands into the linoleum. I cried until I was exhausted.

"Daddy," I finally said, wrapping my arm around his ankle. "Daddy, I want to go home."

"Oh, please, Leslie."

"I want to come back. I just . . . need to go."

"You need to be alone?"

"I guess."

"Well," he said sadly, "I'll drive you then."

"No. You don't need to."

MY FATHER LOOKED at me through the bus window, his car key on a long plastic coil dangling from one hand. The sun, grown hazy, fell flatly across his face. We waved briefly; he receded out of sight. There was just me.

I wasn't sure being alone was really what I wanted.

But I didn't often ride buses, and now I enjoyed sitting high up, suspended above the traffic. I enjoyed the stream of unfamiliar images outside my window, a stream in whose flow I could become submerged without caring.

TEN

"Y ou can see the leaves,"
said Grampa Cole, gesturing toward the photograph
hanging on his wall. The maple tree outside his hospital
window was reflected in the frame's glass. We'd driven
him to the emergency room that morning, after he'd
collapsed on his way up for the mail. It was our first
summer in Connecticut without my father coming out
on weekends.

My grandmother got up to lower his bed. "Are
you comfortable, dear? I want you to be comfortable."

She was continually adjusting his bed as well as
his pillows. At home, she would complain about how

helpless he had become, how he would put on two un-matching shoes or his best Sunday jacket with his old gardening pants if she didn't lay out his clothes every morning. But since he'd been admitted for pneumonia she couldn't do enough for him.

Grampa Cole held onto the bed's railings as if to keep from falling.

"You *can* see the leaves, can't you?" said my mother, gazing at the photograph.

"We should be going inside soon," said Grampa Cole. "It's getting cool. And Mother will be calling us in for dinner."

"Can we eat in the playroom again?" my mother asked.

"Marion . . . please," said Gramma June.

My mother looked down at her lap, smoothing her skirt. The "playroom" had been where my great-grand-mother had dinner served to Grampa Cole and his sister, Mary, on nights when their father came home late. Gramma June didn't like when my mother "encouraged his lapses." My mother thought that it must be wonderful to have all your loved ones come alive, to be surrounded by them once again.

"You're not outside, dear," said Gramma June, pull-ing up his blankets.

He watched her hands smooth and tuck as I'd seen him watch his newest order of chicks scurry around their box. He'd watch for hours at a time, moving only to adjust the light bulb warming them or to spoon out seed from their water. It was Gramma June now who actually took care of the chickens. She complained about that too, although she didn't become nearly as upset as she used to when occasionally a chicken would wander into the house. "Well, *hello*," she'd say, as she would greeting a neighbor's baby out for a stroll.

At home, when Grampa Cole wasn't watching his chickens, he was prowling around the cellar picking through moldy boxes. One day he found a pair of rusted scissors. He spent the afternoon sitting on the porch steps cleaning them with a piece of steel wool, and I saw how his whole life had become an act of waiting. He used to pull down bittersweet vines and get up on a ladder to clean out the gutters. My father had liked to help Grandpa Cole, especially with the vines, pulling back on the thickest ones so that he was almost suspended.

My father. I'd helped him decorate his apartment, selecting curtains and rugs from Macy's. I'd helped him retile his bathroom floor. I'd become his friend; it was easier now to be his friend than his daughter, than the little girl who once had looked up to him so. But our new friendship left me feeling spent, as if I'd already lived out the best of what we could ever have together. Sometimes I found myself down there in the cellar with

Grampa Cole, wondering at old scythes and garden gloves worn so thin they were rags.

SOMETIMES I MISSED Chip now, or rather I missed how he had cared so much about me. I'd seen him only once this summer, when I'd been riding my bike home from the Farmer's Market where I was working again. He'd pulled up beside me in an old brown pickup truck. He told me, with great pride, how he'd saved up for that truck, and that he was working full-time at the hardware store—he thought he might even be promoted to assistant manager soon. He'd moved into his own place, a studio above someone's garage. He'd grown a scraggly beard.

"You never wrote back," he said, flicking a miniature football that hung from his rearview mirror.

"It's been kind of a weird year," I said, leaning against his truck to keep my balance; I was sitting on my bike, feeling young, wishing I already had my license. "My parents split up."

"I'm sorry," he said, reaching out to touch my arm where I rested it on his open window. "That's a bum deal."

I played with the door lock so that I wouldn't have to move my arm, surprisingly comforted by his touch.

"Why don't you come over for a while," he said. "See my place."

"What about my bike?"

"We can throw it in the back."

I didn't know I'd be so glad to see him. "Okay."

HIS STUDIO FELT like an attic, with a pitched roof and a circular window at either end. The other windows were flush with the floor so that you had to crouch to look out. Along one wall he'd hung his fishing gear, including a spear gun, and I remembered the story he'd told me about how he'd had to get stitches in his hand after "wrestling" with a bluefish and getting cut by its fin. There were also a couple of model planes and a toy yellow construction crane lining one bookshelf. "Some things I guess you can't part with," he said, when I wound the crane's little reel to make the hook move.

I looked out one of the circular windows, at a clothesline. A row of white socks hung drying and in the setting sun they were orange. I felt Chip's hand on the back of my neck, lifting my hair. "I wish you'd written," he said.

I turned around to look at him. His eyes were darker than I remembered, so dark I could hardly make out his pupils. "Why do you like me so much?"

"I just do."

"You don't know me. You don't know a thing about me."

"Well, maybe that's it," he said, running one finger across my lips. "You're a *mystery*." He kissed me, and

I'd hoped that I would feel different this time, that I'd feel as good as I had when Todd had kissed me. I didn't, but I let him lead me to his bed anyway.

"I want to see you," he whispered, reaching for my shirt. "I've never seen you." I didn't stop him as he pulled off my shirt and bra, nor did I stop him when he slid off my shorts and underpants. "God, look at you," he exclaimed, kneeling next to me. "You really are beautiful."

I couldn't help feeling self-conscious, and I yanked up the sheet.

"You're so cute," he laughed. "Still saving yourself, aren't you?" He slipped his hand under the sheet and touched me down there. "What for?"

He asked me that so simply I really did begin to wonder what for, even though I'd never exactly been "saving" myself—I'd very much wanted to sleep with Todd. Still, sex seemed like a turning point to me, as my first period had been, even my first adult tooth—a point where there was no turning back to the way things used to be.

Now there was no turning back, anyway, and for the first time I found myself hoping that Deirdre had been right: that sex really was "no big deal." I wanted there to be one less thing to wonder about. He leaned over me as he had last summer when he'd blocked out the sky, and I said, "Make love to me."

"Make love?"

"I want to do it."

He smiled. "If you want . . ." He sat up and quickly pulled off his shirt and pants. In a moment he too was naked, and I thought he'd slip under the sheet with me. He sat on the edge of thé bed and pulled out a condom from his bedside table. He tore it open and I watched, fascinated, as he rolled it on. It was as if he were rolling it onto something that didn't even belong to him.

But then I began to see things much too clearly— just past him, an upside-down crate piled with tapes and loose tennis balls; on the counter, a steel bowl, a single cactus and a pink tissue box decorated, absurdly it seemed, with daisies. I remembered myself as I had remembered myself at the beach, although not quite in the same way—I was making my first real choice, one that had nothing to do with turning points. It had to do with what I really wanted and didn't want at that moment. I really didn't want to have sex with Chip.

"I can't."

"What?"

"I don't want to do it."

We looked at each other for one long horrible moment. There was a clock ticking somewhere and I looked around, needing to see it. It was a Mickey Mouse alarm clock beside his bed.

He leaned across me. "What the hell's the matter with you?"

"Nothing's the matter—"

"You're just too much of a romantic, you know that? A little kissing here, a little kissing there—"

"Maybe I just never really liked you," I said, pushing him aside so that I could get up. I began putting on my clothes, feeling how he'd grown silent. When I looked back at him, he was reaching for a cigarette. He didn't light it, just balanced it on his knee, and I felt sorry. "I mean, I like you, but maybe not enough."

"You don't have to love the first person you sleep with," he said quietly.

"No . . ." I'd put my bra and shirt back on, but I no longer felt self-conscious, and I paused to look out at the clothesline. The socks had faded to gray, now in shadow. They seemed fragile, quivering there like small wounded things. "I know."

I heard him behind me pulling on his pants. "Come on, finish getting dressed. I'll drive you home," he said.

We drove home in silence. We sat for a moment in my driveway, and I said, "You know, you can call me sometime. We can be friends."

"Yeah," he said, not looking at me but at the little football that swung gently. "Better get your bike out," he said, leaving the truck before I did. I never heard from him again, although sometimes he'd wave as he whizzed by me in his truck when I was biking home.

GRAMPA COLE DRIFTED off to sleep. His fever must have been down, since his face wasn't quite so flushed. It had only been an hour ago when he'd been seeing blackbirds flying out from under his bed. "No blackbirds," the nurse had chirped, giving him two aspirin. "Dust bunnies maybe, but no blackbirds."

"Why don't you two go home?" Gramma June whispered. "All three of us don't need to be here."

"We want to be," I said.

"Mom, why don't *you* go home for a little while and freshen up. We can stay," said my mother.

"Me go home? I wouldn't think of it, Marion."

My mother got up from her gray vinyl chair and walked over to the window. She stared down at the parking lot. "Well. Neither would we."

THAT SUMMER, MY mother seemed always to be getting up and walking away from Gramma June. The other day they were refinishing a chair together, sanding off the old paint, when Gramma June burst out with, "Oh, Marion, what are you going to do? Just what are you going to do now?"

My mother leaned back on her heels. "Can't we just enjoy the summer?"

"You're not thinking about things."

"I don't want to think about it right now."

"It's not all going to go away by not thinking about it. What about a job? And that house? Are you two going to go on living all alone in that house?"

My mother didn't answer her. She was bent over, trying to reach under the seat.

"You know, if you'd only been a little more . . . understanding."

My mother sat up.

"Goodness knows, it hasn't always been easy with Cole, but . . . well, I've always tried to be understanding."

"It was all my fault."

"I didn't say that."

"No, but really. It was. But you know, I was just wondering. If it were Holly whose husband left her, would it be all her fault too?"

"Marion!"

"I was just wondering. Anyway . . ." She unwrapped a new piece of sandpaper, but instead of using it she folded it in half and set it up like a tent on the ground. She stood up. "We'll sell the house and I'll get a job. Then everything will be just fine." She ran inside.

I'd overheard this from the porch where I was flipping through a *New Yorker*, glancing at the cartoons. When Gramma June noticed me there, for a moment we looked at each other. "Well, she does," she finally said. "She just has to think about these things."

Without a word, I went inside to find my mother.

She had gone up to her old bedroom. She sat on her bed trying to untangle a necklace she'd recently found in the back of her vanity drawer. It was a necklace my grandparents had given her for her high school graduation. The pendant was a tiny glass heart. I'd tried to tell her about what I'd learned when I'd first visited my father—that it really hadn't been entirely her fault, that he might very well have left anyway. We'd been eating dinner and she'd stared blankly at me from across the table. Then, smiling down at her food, she'd only said, "Well, you're sweet."

I sat next to her on the bed. "Did you really mean that, about selling the house?"

"I guess it *will* be too big for us."

"I can't imagine living anywhere else."

She let her hands drop heavily into her lap. "I can't imagine either." She laid out the necklace across the spread. "It's hopeless. I'll just have to buy a new chain." She got up and wandered around the room, picking up things and putting them down.

There were moments like these when my father felt farther away than he did at others, when he felt as remote as Africa, where he'd recently gone with Clarkson, accompanying her on a dig. I'd already met her, even though he hadn't felt ready for that. I'd insisted, needing to find out whether she was at all an echo of my mother, if maybe subconsciously he was trying to replace her.

She couldn't have been more different from my mother. Clarkson sat with one arm stretched across the back of my father's couch, seeming perfectly at ease in the midst of the papers and dirty laundry strewn across his living room. She wore army boots, something my mother would never wear, and her colors weren't at all my mother's colors, her pants brown and her knee-length shirt a deep red. A thick belt decorated with large silver disks hung around her hips.

Now I wished I'd never met her. Because I could imagine them together. I could imagine him making blueberry pancakes for her on Sunday mornings as he used to for my mother and me, blueberry pancakes, the only thing he knew how to make.

"I suppose I could part with some of these old things," my mother said, holding up a music box. "This doesn't even work and I've still saved it all these years."

"You don't need to start getting rid of stuff," I said.

She tapped the head of the little bear in a tutu. "No?"

I shrugged. "No."

She wound the key in the back of the box. The bear spun slowly. "No music. But he still can dance."

GRAMPA COLE SLEPT soundly. My mother came away from the window. "Why don't we go down to the coffee shop? We could all probably use a cup of tea, don't you think?"

"You two go ahead," said Gramma June. "You can bring me a cup."

"He's asleep. I really think he'll be all right for a

few minutes . . ." said my mother, twisting the opal she now wore on her wedding finger.

Gramma June sighed. "Well, for a few minutes. I guess it would be good for me to stretch my legs."

The coffee shop was almost empty. The big woman behind the counter barely moved from where she leaned against the orange and grape drink machines, immersed in a novel. I kept seeing my grandfather. He'd hit his head when he'd fallen and blood had trickled down around his ear. He had tried to put his shoes back on as he lay on the gurney in the emergency room, insisting that he was fine. His eyes, now baby blue from cataracts, had been wide with fear. Gramma June, gently taking his shoes from him, had said, "You're not *dying*, Cole," even though her hands had trembled.

I folded back the edges of a sugar packet to frame a picture of a trumpeter swan.

"This isn't a bad little café, for a hospital, that is. It's really rather cute," said my mother.

"The house must be a mess," said Gramma June. "We even left the breakfast dishes. And I don't remember if we locked it. Did we lock the house?"

"I did, Gramma June."

She patted my hand. "What would we do without you?"

My mother pressed her spoon into the tea bag on her saucer.

Gramma June shook her head. "I didn't see this coming. I didn't see him getting sick."

"Daddy's not the type to complain," said my mother.

Gramma June stared into her tea. "He looks so . . . old."

"It's those awful white gowns they make them wear. They wouldn't be flattering on anyone."

"I forget that. That we're getting old."

"Oh, Mother, don't talk like that."

"Look at my knuckles." Gramma June made a fist. "Look at those knobby knuckles. These arthritic hands."

My mother looked away. "Please."

"You can't even face up to that, can you?" Gramma June touched my mother's arm. "My poor, sweet girl. Who's going to take care of you?"

"Can't you leave her alone?" I said. "Can't you leave her alone for a minute?"

Gramma June looked at me in surprise.

My mother pushed back her chair. "We should get back to Daddy, don't you think? He might have woken up."

Gramma June squinted at her watch. "Oh, yes. We've been gone too long."

GRAMPA COLE HAD made his way around the bed, leaning on the wall for support. He'd managed to drag the IV to where the pole had fallen across the end of his bed and he'd partially pulled away the bandages securing the needle.

Gramma June rushed over to him. "Cole!"

"I was just going up for the mail."

"The mail can wait. Oh, we shouldn't have left him for a minute, I knew we shouldn't have. And where are the nurses? Why isn't that nurse taking better care of him? Marion, go get the nurse."

Before we left for the night, the nurse had to strap him in. She covered him with what looked like a large bib and wound its ties around the bed. "We can't have you trying to escape us anymore, pumpkin."

"It's not pumpkin," Gramma June snapped. "It's Mr. Creel. Cole D. Creel."

"I don't need this," said Grampa Cole, tugging on the bib. "Oh, I really don't."

"I'm sorry, sweetie," said Gramma June, sounding close to tears. "It's for your own good, you know that."

He nodded vaguely. "You don't have to go. You can stay here. I'm sure they have other rooms."

When I was little and we'd go swimming, my grandfather would carry my grandmother into the water, past the rocky area. She had tender feet. Once they got out where the bottom was sandy, he would gently swing her around, creating the smallest wake, before he'd let her go. I thought about that as Gramma June took his head between her hands. He looked up at her as he had looked up at the sky when we were putting him into the car to go to the emergency room. He'd pointed to the thin path of a plane and said, as if he'd never see the sky again, "What a funny cloud. Oh, what a wonderful, wonderful tail of a cloud."

Gramma June kissed his forehead, holding her lips there. "I'll be back first thing in the morning. I promise."

"Look at this mess," said Gramma June, when we got home. "I can't go to bed until we tidy up a bit."

"I'll catch up on those dishes," said my mother.

"We might as well clean the whole house while we're at it," said Gramma June.

"The whole house?" I said. "Now?"

"It won't take long, between the three of us. If you quickly run the vacuum around, I'll strip the sheets. Marion can do the kitchen."

I thought that cleaning the house would be the last thing I felt like doing. But, surprisingly, I welcomed the whir of the vacuum, the clatter of dishes and the sound of Gramma June moving the beds away from the walls. I even vacuumed the furniture without having to be asked. We could have been preparing for my cousins when they all came at Christmas.

"I'm going to quickly throw these in the machine," said Gramma June, coming downstairs with an armful of sheets.

When we had finished, we sat around the kitchen table drinking glasses of ginger ale. We'd even swept out the fireplace and cleaned the hall closet. "Well, I'm glad that's done," said Gramma June. She ran her finger down the side of her glass. "I wonder if there's anything I could bring him tomorrow. He already has his slippers."

"A puzzle," I suggested. "That might keep him in bed."

"That's a good idea. One of those little puzzles he can fit on his tray. We could probably buy one down in the gift shop."

We were quiet. There was only the soft buzz of the dryer.

"Did you hear that?" Gramma June asked.

"Hear what?" asked my mother.

"Shhh."

"I don't hear anything," I said.

Gramma June got up and switched on the porch light. She leaned her head out the back door. "Hello!" she called. Through the open door I could hear the drip of water from the leaves.

My mother smiled knowingly at me and then I remembered; after my father had first moved out, we'd heard things too. There always seemed to be someone lurking outside. We'd prowl around our backyard with flashlights, peering into the bushes. We never thought to call the police, I think because we knew deep down that it was only our imagination. That it would be a while before we could listen to the silence of the house without feeling that somewhere we'd left a window open or a door unlocked.

"There's no one out there, Mother," she said.

"How do you know? I swear I heard someone. Hello!"

My mother got up. She switched off the porch light. "There just isn't."

Gramma June turned around then, looking bewildered. "Oh. Oh, dear."

My mother fixed Gramma June's collar in the same way I'd only ever seen her fix mine. "Daddy will be coming home."

"I know. Of course he will. But . . ." Gramma June moved over to the sink and picked up a sponge. "I'm losing him." She made as if to wipe the counter, then dropped the sponge into the sink. Facing us, she asked, her hands hanging open at her sides, "What if one day he doesn't know who we are? What if one day . . . he just doesn't know who I am?"

My mother leaned back against the counter, looking down at her shoes.

"Oh, I know that he's always been off in his own world anyway, even before his mind started to go," said Gramma June. "Sometimes even when he held me, I'd feel how far away he was. But he always came back from drifting off, giving me a little squeeze . . . he never for a moment really forgot me." She massaged her temples as if to keep herself from crying. "What would I do if he forgot me?"

"You'd go on loving him," said my mother. "He'd still want you loving him." She flicked the bottle cap from the ginger ale across the counter so that it rang sharply against the sugar canister. "Think about that."

Gramma June shook her head. Then, moving over to her, she lay her hand on my mother's. "Dale has hurt you so, hasn't he?"

I knew how hard my mother could work toward a moment like this, when Gramma June was suddenly all there for her. But she withdrew her hand. She gathered herself that way, as she now would at home after she'd find herself staring out through her own reflection while pulling down the shades for the night. "I'm all right."

"Are you?"

"We should call Holly, don't you think?"

Gramma June's hand stayed where my mother had left it. "Yes," she sighed. "I suppose we should. But can't it wait until tomorrow?"

MY GRANDFATHER DID come home. And after a few weeks he was able to walk up for the mail again, the neighbors calling as usual when they occasionally found him sitting on their lounge chairs or pouring himself a glass of apple juice from their refrigerators; while he could remember our street well enough, all the houses had begun to look the same to him.

He didn't remember being in the hospital at all. He didn't remember his fear of dying, absorbing himself once again in his chickens, provoking the roosters with his foot so that the feathers would rise on their necks and they'd flap their shimmering wings. We too seemed to forget, or at least we tried to. I, for one, didn't want to be reminded of the suddenness with which our expectations of feeding the chickens, mail and going to the dump, of all the basics around which we structured and secured our days, could be shattered.

Still, things weren't quite as they'd always been. Gramma June no longer bothered my mother about the divorce. If she mentioned it at all, it was to criticize my father. "He'll be sorry," she would say, shaking her finger at no one in particular, at the vacuum nozzle as she changed the brushes. "You never know what you've got until it's gone."

Neither did she mind when one day my mother admitted that she never had really enjoyed going to the dump. In fact, she loathed it, the way the wind blew newspapers and Styrofoam cups around her ankles. "Well, that's your right, dear," Gramma June had said, although she'd sounded hurt.

My mother continued going to the dump with her anyway, but not without cheerfully complaining that Gramma June "couldn't lift those dirty old broken tables and chairs she insists on dragging home all by herself."

ELEVEN

he Indian Lake house seemed particularly run down to me when my mother and I went up there toward the end of August. The kitchen walls, once a bright lemon yellow, had faded to a greenish gray, darkened by stove grease and fingerprints. Monster stickers from cereal boxes that we had stuck onto the sills years ago had begun to peel off and flapped in the breezes from the open windows. The counters buckled so badly wet glasses set there would quickly slide to the edges. The table's varnish had been worn away from our years of playing jacks and spinning dimes. And when my mother and I had arrived that afternoon, I'd been alarmed by how much farther down the porch had settled, as if the entire house were gradually sinking into the earth. I'd never thought that this place could depress me. Maybe because I'd never thought that I'd be going up to Indian Lake without my father.

"So Mother told me you'd never know Dad's been sick," Aunt Holly said. She stood at the buckling counter seasoning the pike Uncle Ryan had caught that morning. She had planned to come and visit Grampa Cole in the hospital, but Gramma June had told her that it wasn't necessary.

"Well, he gave us quite a scare," said my mother, shredding the lettuce until it was as thin as coleslaw. She sat opposite Joanne and me as we prepared the string beans. It surprised me how easily we could fall back into old routines; Joanne would be going off to college that year. And besides my father not being there, Meg was six months pregnant and unmarried.

"We eating outside?" Meg asked, coming into the kitchen. She looked much older. Her hair was pulled back into a tight braid and she no longer wore makeup. Her eyes seemed surprisingly small without liner and her lips were as pale as her skin. She looked as if she had stayed out of the sun all summer. She wore a blue and white checkered maternity dress with lace cuffs. I never thought I'd see her in anything but miniskirts and revealing tank tops.

"We are," Aunt Holly answered, without looking up. She flipped the fillet into a pan.

Meg stood beside Aunt Holly, opening the silverware drawer. From the back they looked like sisters; they were exactly the same height and build, with those long, lanky legs and sticklike ankles. Aunt Holly's legs seemed especially skinny, a pair of lavender shorts decorated with shooting stars gaping around her thighs. She still wore her hair cropped just above her ears, and it was only the little creases beginning to show at the nape of her neck that gave away the difference in their ages.

Sorting through the drawer, Meg made soft clinking noises with the forks and knives until Aunt Holly moved away from her to the cutting board. Meg looked at my aunt then as if she'd asked a question and was waiting for an answer. With a fistful of silverware, Meg finally left the kitchen.

"She's getting big, isn't she?" said my mother.

"Yes, well . . ." Aunt Holly slammed a knife down through a turnip. "That happens to unwed mothers still young enough to remember their cheerleading routines—their stomachs grow bigger than watermelons."

"You wouldn't have wanted her to . . . not have it at all, would you?"

"She had her whole life ahead of her." Aunt Holly chopped the turnip into smaller and smaller pieces.

"That would have been murder."

"Oh, Marion. You can think so simply."

"There are no more paper napkins." Meg was leaning against the doorjamb with her arms crossed.

Aunt Holly spoke more softly now. "Take those green cloth ones, honey. From the chest in the living room." She sighed. "Doesn't hurt us to use the good napkins once in a while, I guess, to be a little conservationwise."

Remembering what I knew about the tree house and the number of different boys she had sat with at the end of the dock, I wasn't really surprised that Meg had gotten herself pregnant. Her not knowing who the father was didn't surprise me either. What did surprise me was how angry Aunt Holly seemed, how unforgiving; they'd always been so close I'd never thought anything could come between them.

"There they are," Uncle Ryan exclaimed, coming through the back door followed by Jack. We hadn't seen them yet because they'd been in town having Jack's car checked over for his drive to California. Jack was returning to Berkeley where he was premed.

Meg came in. Uncle Ryan patted her stomach. "How're you doing, pretty mama?"

She smiled weakly.

"So did that Rabbit cost a fortune?" Aunt Holly asked.

"Hardly a penny," said Uncle Ryan, raising a finger to his lips as he looked at Jack.

Aunt Holly frowned. "Just a *pretty* penny, I imagine."

"*So . . .*" said Uncle Ryan, moving over to us. He gave me a kiss, then, leaning over my mother, asked gently, "How are you two doing anyway?"

"You look a little tired, Auntie," said Jack, sounding concerned. She still had dark shadows under her eyes.

"I'm okay. We're okay," my mother answered, pulling behind her ear a long strand of hair that had come loose from the false bun she hadn't given up wearing.

"They're fine," said Aunt Holly. "Now you men get out of here. You're all too big for this house. I can't wait for all you kids to leave."

Uncle Ryan laughed. "Sure, you can't."

"I can't. Then maybe I'll get some work done."

"You get plenty of work done." Looking at us, Uncle Ryan said, "When she first went back to school, I fixed her up that nice quiet den? With that nice desk and adjustable chair? And she chose to spread out in the middle of it all anyway, right at the kitchen table."

"Yes, well, that desk was too small. I couldn't spread out at that desk. Anyway, they'll be plenty to keep me busy, what with a baby coming now."

"It was your idea for me to stay home," said Meg, smoothing the lace of one cuff.

"That's because you can't possibly work and take care of that baby all by yourself, sweetheart," said

Aunt Holly. "At least not until he's old enough for day care."

"You don't think I can possibly do anything."

"We have company, girls," said Uncle Ryan, a new note of sharpness in his voice.

"They're not company," said Aunt Holly. "They're family."

My mother poked through her salad.

THAT NIGHT AFTER I'd changed into my nightgown, I wandered around our room looking at the magazine pictures of flowers Aunt Holly had nailed there years ago. In the dark the daffodils had always reminded me of dragon heads. "It's funny to think of Meg being a mother," I said, taking down the rocks. I sat on my cot to look at them, trying to see what had always made me feel they were special.

"She *is* still a girl," said my mother, drawing the curtains.

"What would you do if I got pregnant?"

"If you got pregnant? Well, I'd hope you wouldn't, at least not before you're married, before you have someone to take care of you, but . . ." She examined the fringe on one of the curtains. "Well, a baby is God's gift, don't you think?"

My mother did think "simply," and for a long time I'd found that frustrating. But lately I'd begun to wonder, watching how she was able to become so lost in prayer, or even now, with all that had happened, the way she was still able to smile up at the sky as if she could see something there that I just couldn't. There'd always been so much room in her world for miracles, for a truth larger than facts. I don't think I believed that a baby was a gift from God. But I wished now that I did.

"Oh, dear," my mother exclaimed, as a curtain rod fell. The rod would fall every summer until we remembered to draw the curtains more gently. My father had been the one to snap it back into place.

This time the rod came apart in the middle and the spring rolled away. "This might be broken for good," she said.

"We'll tell Uncle Ryan about it in the morning," I said, replacing the rocks. "The sun comes up on the other side anyway."

"Does it? Well, I'll sleep through anything tonight." She got into the bed and lay close to the edge even though she now had the entire bed to herself. "You were wonderful today, by the way."

I grinned. "Was I? Thanks." I'd driven most of the way up, in the traffic on the expressways. My mother had driven only toward the end, along the quiet back roads.

I lay on my cot which happened to be set up directly

beneath the now bare window. In the moon's white glow the trees bent toward each other conspiringly. The more I wanted to close my eyes, the more I stared into those trees.

"Are you going to be able to sleep there under that window? The moon seems so bright." My mother had propped herself up against her pillows.

"I don't mind."

"Well, you know, there's plenty of room here. If you feel like sleeping in a real bed."

I got into my father's side. I knew from past summers at Indian Lake that my mother always fell asleep flat on her back with her hands folded across her stomach. Tonight she lay on her side with her knees drawn up to her chest, as if she were hiding from the moonlight. I too was used to sleeping on my back. But I found myself mirroring her, comforted by the warmth of my own darkness beneath the sheets.

THE CAMPER THAT my aunt and uncle had bought was parked just to the left of the driveway. I looked up at it from where I lay on the beach. Tan colored with a green trim, it was nicely camouflaged. Weeds had grown up around it and ivy had begun to climb toward the back window. The tires looked flat, as if the camper, like the house, were sinking into the earth.

"Looks like it's been there forever, doesn't it?" said

Joanne. She lay beside me on a towel. She'd begun to take an interest in her looks again, at least she'd begun to wear jewelry, a few silver rings on each hand.

"Has it been used at all?"

Joanne shook her head, sliding a tiny emerald up and down on her pinky. "The plastic's still on the fold-out couch and toilet seat. But Mom and Dad plan to take a trip soon, after the baby's born. Once they feel Meg can be left alone a little. They want to drive out to Seattle."

"Can you feel him kicking?" my mother asked. She and Meg sat next to each other on lounge chairs.

"I'm having trouble sleeping nights—he seems to wake up then," Meg said, lightly dragging her fingertips across her stomach. She wore a suit with a ruffle skirt, the kind I'd seen only my grandmother wear. Pink storks with babies dangling from their beaks formed a chain around the hem.

Aunt Holly was in swimming. She looked over at them.

"He's going to be a boy," Uncle Ryan said. He was emptying the gasoline from one of the outboard motors into a can. They would be closing up the house soon. "I remember that Holly was always up nights with Jack. The pregnancies with the girls were a dream."

"You know, that may be true," my mother said. "Leslie was a dream too. Thank goodness, since I was laid up in bed for so long." She watched Meg's fingers. "Can I feel?"

"Sure. Though he's quiet now."

My mother firmly placed her hand on Meg's stomach. Her face became suddenly illumined, as suddenly as if my father were there and he had surprised her with a bouquet of roses. "I think I feel him."

"Really?"

"Just a slight stirring."

Aunt Holly had come out of the water. Without saying a word or drying herself off, she sat back down in her lounge chair. Water dripped from her fingertips as they hung over the end of the chair arms. She stared at my mother.

My mother lifted her hand away from Meg. She lifted it to her hair and began tucking loose strands back into her false bun.

"DOES YOUR MOTHER really think Meg should have had an abortion?" I asked. Joanne and I were taking a walk in the woods.

"It seems like that," said Joanne. "But she knows as well as anyone that Meg's never had any great ambitions. She wouldn't have gone on to college anyway, probably. I don't know. Dad's much cooler about the whole thing. He's just happy to be having a grandchild." She picked a fern and skimmed off its leaves. "Mom's been kind of weird lately anyway. She can't seem to make up her mind about anything anymore."

This surprised and disappointed me. "Aunt Holly? She always seems to know exactly what she wants."

"Yeah. She *did*. But she can't even figure out if she really wants to go on for her Ph.D. or not. The more time she has, the more distracted she seems."

I stopped to turn over a rotting log. There was a salamander and I caught it, holding it in my palm. Its webbed feet and tail tickled in a way I'd forgotten and I dropped it. "I guess it takes some getting used to, having you all leave."

"I guess. Even though you know she'd never be up front about that, the fact that she might miss us. Not like your mother."

"My mother?"

"Aunt Marion always loved us all so much and wasn't afraid to let us know it."

I thought of the times I'd been so jealous of my cousins, of how Aunt Holly had been able to treat them as equals. I'd never thought that Joanne might actually be jealous of me. But I was reminded now of the summer when Joanne spent so much time alone at that abandoned house. "You've never really gotten along, have you?" I asked.

"Mom and me? *She* thinks so." Joanne laughed. "She thinks she knows everything about me. But she's always assumed too much. Like assuming that I'd be just like Meg—she bought me a pack of condoms when I was only fourteen. I didn't actually do it until this year."

"Really? Not until this year?"

"See? Even you're surprised."

"No, it's just that . . . well, *I* still haven't."

"So what? I mean, what I've never understood is, what's the big rush with something like that anyway?"

"I don't know," I said, feeling closer to Joanne than I had since we'd shared our imaginary tea at that abandoned house.

"So what do you think you'll do now?" Uncle Ryan asked my mother, as he dealt the cards for a game of Hearts.

It had been a long time since she'd played cards with us. But she seemed to have finally run out of projects, having finished the afghan she'd been crocheting for Gramma June before we'd come up to Indian Lake, and she hadn't begun anything new. Since we'd been there, she'd taken to carrying around smooth round pebbles she'd found in their driveway and would roll between her fingers like worry beads. She rolled one now, as deliberately as if she were memorizing its shape. "Well, that's something Mother has been asking all summer too," she said.

"I'm sorry. It's just that we worry a little about you, that's all. It's not easy to be on your own after all these years."

"No . . ." She glanced at her pebble before tucking it into her skirt pocket. She picked up her cards. "I'm not sure what we'll do."

"We'll be all right," I said.

Uncle Ryan smiled sympathetically. "We know that."

"I suppose I should get a job," said my mother, "even though Dale said not to worry about it, for me to take my time. But I haven't worked since before Leslie was born, when Dale was still in school."

"You'd find something," said Aunt Holly. "And it might be good for you, to get a job. It would get you out of yourself. In fact," she said, clapping her hands at a mosquito, "this might be the best thing that's ever happened to you."

A six of diamonds fell from my mother's hand. "What?"

"That's perhaps easier for you to *say*, Holly," said Uncle Ryan.

"Why? She's never been out on her own, she's never had the chance to find herself. So now she does."

"God, Mom," said Meg. "You make divorce sound like some kind of blessing."

"Maybe it is. A mixed blessing."

"Holly." Uncle Ryan frowned at her. "You can be too glib sometimes, sweetheart." For a moment he became much more than the big lovable kid I'd always known him to be, and I was grateful.

Aunt Holly leaned back in her chair. "Why do you all have to treat her like she's about to break? She's always been treated like that. Well, maybe she's a lot tougher than you think."

"He *left* me," said my mother, her eyes suddenly wide and staring. She seemed to have forgotten that she was holding cards at all as more fell from her hand. "Dale left me."

For a long moment Aunt Holly and my mother looked at each other, until it was Aunt Holly who looked away. She straightened the worn corners of her cards. It was the first time I'd ever seen her look the least bit embarrassed.

MY MOTHER WASN'T there when I woke up in the middle of the night, but I could hear voices coming from the kitchen. I crouched in the hall, near the fishing boy sitting on the trunk. He seemed to have his line cast into the light overflowing from the kitchen.

"I just felt somehow . . . that I'd been lifted out of life's stream," I heard Meg say. "And I started thinking, what we're really here for is to live, give lives and die. I mean, when you get down to it, that's really it."

There was the sound of a spoon stirring something in a cup.

"When I was pregnant," said my mother, "I couldn't stop seeing Leslie. She was in my mind's eye whether I was doing the dishes or lying in bed all those months. Not like those pictures of babies in medical books. But as I imagined what a secret would look like."

"So . . . what did it look like, the secret?"

"It's silly."

"Tell me."

I could hear my mother rotating her cup on her saucer as she would now in the mornings when she'd gaze worriedly out the window. "Kind of . . . like blue glass. Blue beach glass you find, soft and milky blue around the edges. Clear as pool water through the middle." They were both quiet until my mother forced a giggle. "I told you it was silly."

"That's beautiful."

"We should be getting back to bed, don't you think?"

I pretended to be asleep when my mother quietly slipped back beneath the covers. She didn't move for a long time and I opened my eyes to look at her. She'd fallen asleep on her back. Her hands were folded peacefully across her stomach, and I saw that there were things I didn't know about her. Things I might never know. Like that image of blue glass, an image she had once created for herself, and for herself alone.

_____

AFTER DINNER SUNDAY night, Uncle Ryan and Jack had to drive back to Syracuse. Jack had to collect some things there before leaving for California and Uncle Ryan had to work the next day.

"You make sure you leave your room there the way you found it," said Aunt Holly, as Jack was putting last-minute tennis rackets and books into his car. "I don't want to have to go back to that house and clean up after you."

"Don't worry, Mom," said Jack, shutting the trunk. "You'll never know we'd been there."

As he was saying good-bye to her she tugged gently on his shirt. "Look at this. I taught you how to sew when you were twelve so you would always be able to sew on your own buttons. So that you could always do for yourself. Now look at you."

"Mom." Jack kissed her forehead. "Since when do you fuss so?"

Aunt Holly pulled at the spot where a button should have been.

When she was saying good-bye to Uncle Ryan, she asked, "Call me tonight, will you?"

"I always call you when I get home."

"I know, of course you do."

He ran one of his mittenlike hands across her short hair. "Did you think I'd forget?"

"Of course not," she said. But she leaned against him as if she wouldn't be seeing him for a very long time.

THEY WERE GONE, Uncle Ryan having driven off in his own car and Jack in his Rabbit with a bumper sticker that said, "I love elephant seals."

After they'd turned the corner, Aunt Holly continued to gaze down the road. She scratched the back of one ankle with her other foot. When she turned around, her eyes were red. "Well, Jack's finally gone. I'm glad he's gone."

Meg slipped her arm through her mother's. "I know."

"Really," said Aunt Holly. "Besides, you know what we can do now? Skinny-dip."

"Skinny-dipping?" asked Meg.

"Why not? It's dark out now, and all the men are gone."

"It's kind of cool with that wind," said my mother.

My aunt was already marching down toward the water.

"I'll get some towels," said Meg wearily.

"Not for me," said my mother. "I'm happy to watch."

I'D NEVER GONE skinny-dipping before. It reminded me of getting into bed and lying naked between the sheets after a shower. But it was also so much more, a feeling of freedom as if I were shedding my body into the lake.

Fully clothed, my mother sat alone on the shore hugging her knees. There was no point in trying to convince her to come in; she'd never shown herself naked to me, let alone my aunt and cousins. Whenever we went shopping together, she would make me wait outside her dressing room.

When I was already getting out, Meg was standing where it was only up to her ankles.

"You're doing it the hard way," called Aunt Holly.

"That's because I'm not sure I want to be doing this in the first place," said Meg.

"It would be good for that baby if you got a little exercise."

"I know what's good for my baby."

Aunt Holly floated on her back and said, as if to herself but loud enough for us to hear, "You don't begin to know."

Meg got out then. She began putting on her clothes. "I'm so tired of this."

"What did I do? What have I done now?"

"It's what you've been doing all summer. Treating me like I'm some kind of complete imbecile. Like I have no idea what I'm doing. Well, I have news for you—this baby wasn't a mistake. I *tried* for this baby."

"What?" Aunt Holly waded in to shore. "You idiot."

"See? That's just like you. That's absolutely just like you. You've always been so big on letting us live our own lives, and that's what I'm trying to do. But you know what? That was just your way of holding on. You don't *begin* to know how to let go!" Bunching her clothes under one arm, she ran back up to the house.

"Meg!" Aunt Holly called.

"Leave her alone, Mom," said Joanne. She was getting out of the water, pulling herself up onto the edge of the dock.

Aunt Holly stood there dripping. She peered out at Joanne as if she couldn't quite see her through the dark.

"Don't you see how you're hurting her?"

In the light Meg had turned on in the house, I was able to see tiny folds of fat just beneath Aunt Holly's buttocks. And just above the folds was a birthmark. It seemed to be smeared there, a smudge of dirt you'd like to wipe away. I suddenly could imagine her examining it, grimacing at herself in the mirror.

She looked back up at the house but then reached for a towel and, wrapping herself in it, sat beside my mother. "I keep hoping for one thing. One selfish thing," she said, bringing up her knees and holding onto her toes. "That it will look just a little bit like me. That when she looks at that baby, she'll still see me."

"I'm sure she will," said my mother. She picked out a small round stone to roll between her fingers.

Aunt Holly pulled her towel more closely around her. She was shivering. "You think so?"

I didn't remember my aunt ever asking for my

mother's opinion on anything. As she turned to look at her sister her mouth fell a little open, and I saw that it was more than an opinion she wanted. It was assurance.

"Well, yes," said my mother, sounding embarrassed. Then, tossing the stone into the water, she said, "Yes, I really do."

We all stared at the lake, at the lights from the houses trickling like slow leaks across the water.

"Well, I'll just have to stick my toe in," said my mother, getting up so abruptly she nearly tripped. But she took off more than just her shoes. She took off her skirt and blouse, neatly piling them on a stump.

With her back to us she quickly slipped out of her bra and panties and dashed into the water, but not before I could see her—she wasn't nearly as shapeless as I'd always imagined, her breasts and hips defined enough so that she seemed gently sculpted. She was beautiful, not just in the only way I'd ever known, when she'd wear one of her best skirts. She was beautiful in a way it now occurred to me my father must have found deeply alluring.

"It's nice," she called out.

Her voice cracked as it would when she was nervous, and I knew that she didn't think it was "nice" at all. But I loved her so much then—she had dared herself to do something that she'd never done before, that made her feel entirely uncomfortable and even afraid; she was not fond of swimming and would always peer down through the water to see what might be lurking in the lake's depths. Now the water was as black as the sky and she couldn't see a thing. She treaded water in one place, barely disturbing the surface.

TWELVE

It had never occurred to me that Aunt Holly wouldn't know how to let go of her children. And I never thought that I would feel sorry for her. But the following spring when Meg's son, Whitney, was about five months old, they all came to Connecticut, and I remember Aunt Holly dangling a capped pen from the coffee table in front of him as he lay on the couch. Meg snatched it away, saying, "Don't you know babies shouldn't play with pens?"

I had expected Aunt Holly to frown. Instead, she'd looked hurt, busying herself with pulling up Whitney's socks. By then Meg had started working behind a cosmetics counter and Whitney had just begun day care, but Aunt Holly had convinced Meg to go on living at home. "She might as well save her money on rent that way," she'd explained, trying to comb the baby's downy hair with her fingers.

Around that same time, my mother started working part-time in a bookstore. We also moved into an apartment, and every night I'd wake to the clock that used to hang in our downstairs hall and think I was back in my room with the window seat. My mother would be up nights too. I'd hear the padding of her slippers as she paced the apartment or the crumpling of newspapers as she unpacked one of the boxes still piled in the hall. Mostly she unpacked only as she needed things, her mixing bowls one morning when she decided to make pancakes, her sewing basket when I lost a button. It would be a long time before we emptied all those boxes.

The dark blue floral couch loomed out from our new off-white living room. Back in the old house it had blended with the blue walls. The highboy looked particularly large and cumbersome squeezed next to the little pine desk that had been in our den. Often when I looked at these things now, I barely recognized them. When I was alone in the apartment, I found myself marveling at the detail of the coffee table's feet or the brass knobs of the hall chest, things I'd never noticed before.

Even those things that hadn't changed, like school, seemed different; in class I'd steal glimpses at my friends and notice things about them as I would with our furniture, as if I'd never really known them at all. Todd was in a lot of my classes and sometimes I'd watch him as I used to watch him backstage. But I'd begun to wonder what exactly I'd loved so much about him.

I lived as near to school as I always had but now walked there from an entirely different direction, past three-family houses or buildings like our own with cement courtyards. One day I heard someone running up behind me, and I should have known from the heavy slap of her feet that it had to be Elsa, a girl I'd known since grade school. She'd run like that down the halls, bouncing a soccer ball even though she didn't play soccer.

She was wearing a beaded yellow and green vest over a tie-dyed jumpsuit, and a pair of cat red-rimmed sunglasses. Unlike me, who still wore my hair flipped back like the rest of the high school girls, gold rings on my index fingers, and tight jeans.

"What are you doing around here?" she asked, tossing back her long, thick red hair. Her freckled face looked small beneath it.

"I live around here."

"No, you don't."

"You know it all, don't you?" I walked a little faster. "We moved."

"Oh, that's right—your parents got divorced."

"Thanks for clearing that up."

"Sorry, really."

Elsa and I had never really been friends. She'd just been someone who had always been around; at those end-of-year parties my mother gave she'd play by herself in a corner of the yard with a hula hoop until my mother persuaded her to join the others, letting her be the first up at bobbing for apples. She'd never been able to fit in, mostly because she never seemed to want to; she was always drawing attention to herself as being different, from the way she dressed to how she got in trouble for sneaking into the auditorium so that she could hold her own private séances beneath the stage. But the teachers excused her behavior since she always got straight A's. She'd been known for handing in papers scribbled on paper bags rolled into scrolls and doing better than the rest of us who'd been up all night typing.

"I guess you're living with your mother then," she said. "I mean, it's rarely the father who gets custody."

"You know an awful lot, don't you?"

"Just speculating. Well, see you later." She walked off into the parking lot of a kindergarten building.

"You can't get to school that way," I said.

"I'm not going to school."

I noticed now that she wasn't carrying any books, only her sketch pad that I knew, from her doodling in class, was filled with boats.

"Where are you going then?" I asked.

"Nowhere."

"You can't be going nowhere."

"Well, nowhere special anyway. I mean, it's special to *me* but wouldn't be to anyone else. . . . Why do *you* care where I'm going anyway?"

"I don't."

"I bet you've never cut school in your entire life."

There was a small cluster of dandelions at my feet. I tried to break off their heads with my heel.

"You can come if you want," she said.

"Why would I want to?"

"Because. You're still standing there."

ELSA SAT ON the school bus steps, her hair a brilliant orange in the sun. The bus was one of two abandoned and hidden among the trees behind the parking lot. All that remained of the seats were their springs. The doves that roosted in the other bus didn't seem to mind our being there, scratching uninterruptedly among the dandelions and red shards of broken taillights.

"I bet you've never hung out in a place like this."

I sat on the metal rim of the driver's seat. The windshield was gone, so that leaves fell into the bus. "Why would I want to hang out in a broken-down old bus?"

"Because. No one would think to find you here. Right now, no one in the world knows where you are."

I remembered the abandoned house at Indian Lake, how no one had known where we were then.

"I have to admit," said Elsa, opening her pad, "you're the last person I'd expect to grace my presence." She unwound a rubber band from around her colored pencils and laid them out across the step. "I mean, you've always hung out around Deirdre. *She* wouldn't be caught in my presence—I'm not nearly popular enough."

She was right about Deirdre, so there wasn't anything I could say to that. Deirdre and I no longer spent so much time together, since she now had a steady boyfriend. She claimed to be "in love," and I wondered if she shared with him all those secrets she'd only ever really shared with me. I sometimes wondered now what had made us such good friends.

I propped my chin on my hands, folding them over the steering wheel. "I don't know why I'm here either."

Through the branches I could just see the playground, the canvas swings and the seesaw cutting a sharp angle against the bright blue wall of the kindergarten building. It was meant to be a kind of ocean mural, something the children themselves must have done, with crookedly outlined fish and grinning crabs.

"You know, it's not the end of the world that Todd didn't end up liking you," said Elsa. "I mean, if that's why you're here—to avoid him."

"I told you—I don't *know* why I'm here. And that was all a long time ago anyway."

She drew quietly, her pencil moving slowly across the page.

"How did you know about Todd?"

She frowned. "It was a little obvious the way you followed him around."

"God."

"Don't worry. No one really noticed but me." She picked out another pencil. "I study these things. Anyway, it never would have worked—you two are as opposite as the sun and rain."

"Opposites attract."

"Yeah, but do they stay together?"

It annoyed me how easily she was able to dismiss him. "Maybe you're just a little jealous."

I was hoping I'd make her angry, but instead she laughed. "No, I'm not jealous, Leslie," she said patiently. "I'm just intelligent enough to know that someone like that isn't going to be particularly interested in someone like me. And I'm willing to wait around for someone who is."

It must have been morning recess. The children streamed out of the building, in their bright pink and blue sweaters, quickly filling the slide and swings. I felt as if I were watching them from the inside of a window, as I used to watch the neighborhood kids walking home from school when I was sick. The quiet of my room would settle heavily around me as the plaintive cooing of the doves did now. I looked back at Elsa. I could see now that what she'd been drawing was another boat and I wished suddenly I could be like that, so driven. Then maybe I too would be more willing to wait around for that someone who would like me for who I really was.

"Why is it that's the only thing you draw, boats?" I asked.

"Because. One day I'm going to build my own boat and sail across the Pacific."

I laughed. "I should have guessed."

She looked at me for what seemed the first time since she'd opened her sketchbook. "You don't believe I can do that only because you can't imagine doing anything like that yourself. And you can't imagine because you've been conditioned to believe there are limits."

"Is that your philosophy of life or something?"

"No. Just a fact. About you and most people."

"There *are* limits. Practical ones anyway."

She didn't answer me, looking back at her drawing. She shaded in an area that looked like a satellite dish. "So what do *you* want to do?" she asked.

"With my life? I don't know. I've thought about going to law school."

"Anything else?"

"I don't really know. Maybe I'll become a biologist or an engineer." I had trouble looking too far into the future.

"Interesting. So there we have your practical list. So

what are the things you've thought about doing but never really seriously considered? How about designing a watertight ventilated dome so that we can live under the ocean?"

"What?"

"It's possible."

"Maybe, but no. No, I've never thought about doing anything like that."

"Grafting a breed of snapdragons that could be grown on the moon?"

"Never," I laughed.

"Learning to fly?"

"To fly?"

"But without wings. Just you."

"This is a stupid conversation."

"You have, haven't you?"

"As a kid, yes. Haven't we all?"

"Sure, as kids. But I bet you think about it even now. What it would feel like if those few seconds after, let's say, diving off a board into a pool, when you haven't begun to fall yet but are still in the air . . . what it would feel like if those few seconds could last a little longer."

I used to love diving off the raft into Indian Lake. The part I hated most was how quickly the surface would close over me. "That's something that's not even as possible as building boats."

"You're so technical. All right, we'll give you wings,

then. So that you can hang-glide. You could teach hang gliding, how about that?"

"All right. I could do that."

She grinned. "You could?"

"I could *imagine* doing it anyway."

"There's hope for you yet." She grinned at me, for a moment pulling back her hair so that I could see her full face. Her features were surprisingly delicate and I realized I'd never really looked at her before. She was pretty. "You really plan to do that, don't you, build your own boat," I said.

She laughed. "And you thought I was dreaming."

ONE SUNDAY I was helping my mother make a collage of dried flowers. We'd picked the flowers on the way home from church, detouring past the field near our old house where we used to fly kites. For a while I'd regularly spent weekends at my father's place and wouldn't have been home until late Sunday afternoon, but it had been a strain on both of us. We'd take day trips into New York City, to go to concerts or to the Museum of Modern Art. I'd begun spending fewer weekends over there, especially now that he was spending more time with Clarkson. We were both more comfortable with an occasional dinner together, or a movie.

My mother and I had the flowers spread out across the kitchen counter and were weeding through them for the least broken ones when my mother said, "You know, I've been meaning to tell you . . . there's someone I would like to have over for dinner. Someone I met. At the bookstore."

I looked at her. "Someone you've been . . . seeing?"

"He was just there one day at the register and we started talking. A few days later he asked me to lunch." She laughed. "Lunch, can you imagine? No one's asked me out like that since your father first asked me for an ice cream soda after school."

"He's not married?"

She smiled as I hadn't seen her smile since my father. "He told me he's just never met the right woman."

"What's his name?"

"Leonard. Leonard Miller. He's really very knowledgeable, reminds me of your father that way. He's even studied philosophy extensively. And he's very sweet. He treats me like such a lady. He has a way of making me feel like . . ." She seemed about to save a flower but then tossed it aside. "Well, like your father used to."

Her face became pinched in that way it would now when she was doing things she usually enjoyed. One morning she was repotting a geranium out on our balcony when I saw that look. I saw how much she knew. That my father had ultimately outgrown her. That she could never measure up to Clarkson, whom she'd accidentally met at the cleaners when my father was picking up a pair of pants. She had looked up from her geranium, her mouth freezing into a brilliant smile. "Isn't this the most beautiful pink? It's called Picasso pink."

I gazed at a stalk of milkweed, wondering how a flower could end up with such a wooden shell. "Sounds like you've been seeing each other for a while."

"Oh, not really. Just a few weeks."

"A few *weeks*?"

"It's never been for anything more than lunch, Leslie."

"What does he do? For a living?"

"He makes cabinets."

"Cabinets?"

"Yes, cabinets. Anyway, I'd like for you to meet him."

"I don't need to meet him. I mean, if you're not ready for that."

"I know you don't need to. But I'd feel better if you did."

The counter was littered with dried brown flowers. "What are we going to do with this thing anyway, once we finish it?" I asked.

"We'll hang it," she said. "In the dining area."

The "dining area" was the corner where we'd set up the kitchen table. We kept our television on top of our old dining room table where it could only fit folded against one wall. Beneath it were tucked more boxes we hadn't yet unpacked.

IT WAS HARD to imagine my mother actually meeting someone, but then I remembered how surprised I'd been by her the first time I'd visited her at the bookstore. I'd dropped by one day after school and had expected the store to be shadowy and quiet. I'd expected the books to smell musty from sitting so long on the shelves with only an occasional customer dropping by, and essentially my mother would have nothing to do; she'd spend most of her time staring out the window, and people on the sidewalk would see her as I'd seen her from our yard when my father had cut down that tree.

Instead, the store was brightly lit by fluorescent lights and my mother was serving a long line of people at the cash register. She smiled pleasantly as the customers slapped down their books and didn't seem to mind if they didn't smile back, and it occurred to me that she was better able to overcome her shyness behind a counter. She didn't notice me as I came and stood at a little distance, where I could watch as she worked the cash register. Her fingers moved quickly, knowingly, across the keys, and I was amazed; for so many years she'd retold those stories about having to work as a cashier at the A&P when my father was in school that they'd seemed like nothing more than just that—stories. I'd never been able to envision her actually working.

When she'd taken care of the last person in line, I came around to the front of the counter. "Leslie!" she exclaimed, obviously expecting me to be just another customer. A stern, balding man came up to her, saying, "Marion, the rush seems to be over, so feel free to take a short break."

"Mr. Martin, I'd like you to meet my daughter."

He looked at me rather disinterestedly over a pair of glasses so small they reminded me of the double-ended blower from a bottle of bubbles. Without any change of expression, he said, "Your mother's a lifesaver."

WE WENT NEXT door for cups of ice cream and sat outside on one of the benches beneath an awning.

"Mr. Martin seems pretty happy with you," I said.

"Well, I hope so. But it's such a nice surprise, having you just drop by like this," she said, sounding very pleased.

We wound our spoons around and around until we'd sharpened the ice cream into peaks, the way we'd always eaten ice cream together, and I asked, "When you used to work, you know, back when Daddy was in school . . . did he ever just stop by?"

She speared her spoon into her ice cream and rested the cup on her knee, and the question seemed to have taken on more weight than I'd intended. "No. He never did," she said. "At least not that I remember . . ." She looked at me, explaining, "He was so busy, you know, with his studies. He couldn't help it."

I remembered how I'd felt that night I'd heard her confiding in Meg about her secret of blue glass. How I'd realized then that there were things I just didn't know about my mother. Now I knew that there were things even my father had never known about her. Things that maybe he could have known if he'd only taken the time. If he'd only once dropped by to see her.

I WAS CURIOUS about Leonard, but at the same time I dreaded meeting him and I wasn't sure why. Maybe because I expected him to feel as if he had to impress me, like Clarkson seemed to feel; she was always trying to please me with presents of blouses that she thought were in fashion.

On the night when he was coming over for dinner, my mother quickly tidied up the bathroom. "Women's personal habits are terribly important to men, you should remember that. They'll notice all those little things like hairs in the sink." She squatted in her favorite dinner dress to scrub the base of the toilet. She held the pink lace hem between her legs.

"He's going to notice things down there?" I stood in the doorway wrapped in a towel. She'd been waiting for me to get out of the shower.

"He might look," she said, straightening and shaking

out her skirt. "Men can't help looking, it's just how they are. And they can't help holding those little things against you."

"Did Daddy do that, examine our toilets?"

She looked at herself in the mirror as she rinsed out the sponge. "I don't know what Daddy did. But I do know he didn't leave me for how I kept our bathrooms. I kept them spotless. I kept them clean."

Her face became pinched again. When she saw me looking at her in the mirror, she said, "So what do you think, should I wear my hair down?"

Before I could answer she was already pulling out the pins from her false bun. She laid the bun on the sink. The ends of her shoulder-length hair curled slightly from having been so tightly twisted. But she looked suddenly so fresh and unworried I was as disarmed by her as I had been that night when we'd all gone skinny-dipping. Her sharp features seemed more dramatic, less severe now.

"You look amazing," I said.

She let her hair fall across one eye so that she could comb it back with her fingers. She let it fall again, as if practicing. As if trying to remember the way she used to be.

"Oh, Leslie, do get dressed," she said, looking at her watch. "Leonard will be here any minute. And I'd better check the lamb. I'm afraid it may be cooking too fast.

That always happens to me," she said, rushing out of the bathroom.

"I don't think you want to leave this lying around, Mom," I said, picking up the bun.

"Oh." She took the bun, for a moment stroking it. "I hope you like him."

I shrugged. "It's you who has to like him."

She touched my cheek. Then she said, "Put on that rose dress, why don't you."

MY MOTHER HAD compared Leonard to my father so, I expected to be reminded of him. Perhaps they looked a little alike in that they both had that rough, unshaven look, but Leonard wore a leather jacket while my father would have worn a blazer with patches on the elbows. I was most surprised by how much younger he seemed, maybe in his early thirties. I'd never thought that my mother would be going out with a younger man, one who even wore a gold chain around his neck like some of the guys at school wore. And he was good-looking, as my father had been good-looking, but in a much more rugged way.

He handed my mother a bouquet of yellow roses.

"Oh, how did you know these were my favorite?"

"You'd happened to mention it."

My father had always given her yellow roses.

"Your hair. It looks nice," he said, gazing at her as if captivated.

"Thank you," she said, once running her hand through it as she had in the mirror. "I'd like you to meet Leslie."

He smiled at me. "Well, you're as lovely as your mother."

I looked at my shoes, feeling as I had the last time I'd worn that dress, to a wedding of a friend of my father's from graduate school. He led me around by the hand as if I were a little girl, introducing me as "my Leslie." I was embarrassed but he'd known I was embarrassed; he gave me winks and little squeezes of the hand. I tried not to smile, not to buckle under his adoration.

My mother ushered us into the living room, her dress rustling. "So what would you like to drink, Leonard?"

"Beer would be fine if you have it," he said, watching my mother as she moved swiftly around the room plumping up the pillows and straightening the doilies. She was radiant.

"Beer? Yes, I did pick up some beer. And Leslie, I'll bring you a ginger ale. Now you two sit, while I put these in water. I have to get out the dips too. The celery is chilled so I didn't want to put it out because it might become limp. I have to check the lamb."

"Do you need help?" I asked.

"No, sweetheart. You just sit, keep Leonard company."

When she'd left the room, he sat at the far end of

the couch absently fingering one of my mother's needle-point pillows. "You have a nice place here," he said.

I sat opposite him and dug my hand into one of the bowls of nuts my mother had scattered around the room. "We still have some unpacking to do."

He nodded, glancing for a moment at the collage that we hadn't yet hung, only propped up beside the television. From a distance it looked like a muddy brown painting. "Unpacking can take forever." He smiled kindly. "It can be easier, I guess, to live out of boxes."

My mother returned balancing the platter of dips and a tray of drinks. "Have you gotten a chance to get acquainted?"

"You were only gone a minute, Mom."

"I was just saying what a nice place you have," said Leonard.

"It is nice," said my mother, sitting beside him. "At least the plumbing works. The plumbing never worked back home. But this building's so new. Some of the stickers were even on the windows. And the closet doors. I can't get used to sliding closet doors." She dabbed her lips with a tightly balled cocktail napkin. "No, the plumbing never worked at home. And that chimney, remember that, Leslie? Every rain it leaked—came right through the wall. The house was falling apart."

"Sounds like my house."

"Oh, but your house sounds wonderful. And you

know how to fix things. He's even put in a skylight," she said, briefly looking at me. "Has completely renovated it himself, imagine that."

He gazed admiringly at her.

She broke off a piece of cracker, eating it plain. "You actually build the cabinets in a studio at your house, don't you?"

"Not exactly a studio. The garage."

The apartment was suddenly so quiet I could hear the bathroom faucet dripping.

My mother got up then. "That lamb must be almost done. And I should let it cool a few minutes. It tastes better cooled."

I was angry with her for disappearing again. We listened to her in the kitchen, the oven door opening and closing, until he said, "You look like your mother."

"People say I look more like my father."

He smiled the way he had before, kindly. Sympathetically. "I guess I just haven't met your father."

I wondered if it was wrong to mention my father at all. "So my mother said you've studied philosophy."

He laughed. "Did she? Well, I haven't exactly *studied* it. I just pick it up once in a while. Like I pick up poetry. Or science fiction. I just like to read."

"Oh." I dug my hand into the nuts.

"I hope I haven't disappointed you."

"What? No . . . I'm not disappointed. I mean, *I* don't read philosophy. It seems kind of pointless anyway, proving that you exist, that kind of thing."

"Sometimes it does, doesn't it?" He nodded thoughtfully. "Sounds like your father has studied quite a bit though, having gone to graduate school and all."

"She talks about him to you?"

"Occasionally. It doesn't bother me if it doesn't bother you—he sounds like an admirable man."

"It doesn't bother me. I just didn't expect that she would, that's all."

"She was very much in love with him."

I must have looked taken aback, because he added, "That's not something she told me. I've discovered that for myself."

I wondered if she could hear us, but she'd shut the kitchen door as she used to at home to keep the steam from buckling the wallpaper, even though we had no wallpaper here.

"Your mother tells *me* you're very good on the guitar."

I laughed, realizing my mother had exaggerated me to him just as much. "No, not really. I've just taught myself a few chords."

"Do you write your own songs?"

"Sometimes. More like lines—I used to write poetry."

"I'd love to hear you play sometime."

"I don't really play for anyone, not even my mother—she just hears me through my door."

I thought he'd persist, but all he said was, "Well, your own audience is as good as any. Unless you're looking to become famous, if you're dependent on praise that way."

"You never wanted that?" I asked.

"To be famous? I suppose," he shrugged. "But I guess never enough to pursue any one thing." He laughed. "Besides building cabinets, anyway, and you can't become too famous at that. But I'm lucky. I'm able to make a living at what I love doing most. I've always loved building things."

I realized then that there was nothing at all special about this guy. But neither was he trying to impress me by pretending to be special, to be something he wasn't. Even though maybe in my mother's mind he was like my father. He seemed entirely comfortable in his lack of ambition, and in that sense seemed to know himself well.

"Do you think we should go help your mother?"

"In the kitchen?"

"Is that not allowed?"

My father had never helped in the kitchen. "She might be surprised, but, sure. We can help."

———

IF I STARED at the grinning crabs long enough, they seemed to move slowly across the kindergarten wall. "My mother's seeing someone."

"Great." Elsa adjusted the green felt hat she wore so that it shaded her eyes as she leaned over her pad. There was a peacock feather tucked into its band.

"I keep thinking, though, they're hardly divorced."

"Is your father seeing anyone yet?"

"Actually, he is."

"Then what's the big deal?"

"I don't know. I can imagine my father with someone else. But I guess I could never imagine my mother."

"He left her, huh?"

I tossed out a leaf through the open windshield, watching as it spun upward and was carried off on a breeze. "Yeah."

"So do you like this guy?"

"I've only met him once, but he seems nice. Yes, I like him. He seems . . . laid back. I like that."

"So *that's* what's bothering you," she said, looking up at me. A scarf was attached to the hat so that it could be tied under the chin. But instead of tying it she'd fastened it with a rhinestone pin, the kind my grandmother would pick up at a garage sale and end up tossing into one of her baskets. "You should be glad you like him. I mean, think what it would be like if you didn't and he ends up hanging around all the time. My mother's gone out with dozens of guys—"

"Your mother? Your parents are divorced?"

"Yes. I mean no." She shifted on the step. "My mother and her second husband, Garry, divorced. My own father died. Anyway, she's gone out with all these men, and I've never really liked any of them. But she had the best kid with Garry. Audrey's only four but smart as anything."

I'd never known that about Elsa, that her father had died. I thought back to those parties, remembering how she'd played alone with the hula hoop. She'd roll it across the lawn and watch it until it finally fell. "When did he die, your father?"

"Oh, a long time ago. I was six or seven, I forget." She shut her pad. "Anyway, we don't have to spend the whole day here. And I know where we can go."

WE ENDED UP at a basement thrift shop, lit by dim bare bulbs that made the cement floor look swampy green. A fat gray and white cat slept on top of a heaping basket of "Three Dollars Each" T-shirts. Card tables piled with rumpled sweaters, pants and shirts were set up down the middle of the store. Racks of dresses and jackets lined the walls, except for where there was a large gold-rimmed mirror. And at the end of the store sat an old woman, deeply sunk in a plush chair.

"Hi, Anna!" Elsa yelled.

"Well, there she is," the old woman said, one side of her mouth rising into a smile while the other sagged.

Her lips were sharply outlined in red and she wore large dangling earrings of what looked like gold cupids. Around her thin, wrinkled neck were layered beaded necklaces that were all but lost against the confusing purple swirls of her dress. In her lap was an old painting that seemed to have turned black with age. She was cleaning it with something from a jar she kept on the arm of the chair. One hand held a rag while the other lay curled and motionless in her lap.

"How's that coming?" Elsa asked.

"It's coming, slowly. You got to be real careful." She looked at me. "Someone tossed it out, can you imagine?" She pointed to an area she had already cleaned. "You can just begin to see something there, looks like a weeping willow."

"This is Leslie. She's cutting school too."

"Elsa." I pinched her.

"It's all right," said Elsa, taking off her felt hat to try on a straw one. She looked at herself in a hand mirror from the table beside Anna's chair. "Anna understands."

Anna leaned forward, her chest for a moment hiding the willow. "School made me feel like a caged bird."

"So what new things do you have, Anna?"

"Look at that rack over there. Got some great new sequined things in you might like."

As Elsa rummaged through the rack, I thought how

I could never wear any of those old clothes. Their mustiness combined with the damp smell of the basement depressed me. Anna seemed as absorbed in her painting as Elsa could be in her drawings, gently scrubbing with her rag.

"Yes!" Elsa exclaimed, holding up an emerald-green dress with a full taffeta skirt. "Oh, I hope it fits," she said, going into the bathroom which I guessed was also the dressing room.

While she was changing, Anna looked up, shaking her head. "Elsa. What a special girl."

"Special?"

She let her good hand drop heavily into her lap, looking scornfully at me. "She's so *free*, dear."

Elsa came out in the dress and grinned at herself in the gold-rimmed mirror. "It's a little tight, but I love it!" She swung her hips back and forth so that the skirt rose.

"When would you wear that?" I asked.

She shrugged. "To school."

I laughed. "You would, too."

"Why don't you try something on yourself, dear?" Anna asked, putting aside the painting.

"That's okay."

"Yeah," said Elsa. "You don't have to buy anything. Just pretend—what would you wear if you were to wear what you really like?"

"I like what I'm wearing."

"How can you like jeans? They're just there. You've been conditioned to like them, that's all."

"Oh, like I've been conditioned to think I want to be a lawyer when all I really want is to fly, right?"

"Exactly."

I was suddenly angry at how self-assured she always seemed. "Why are you like this? Why do you have to be so different?"

"I don't have to be. I want to be."

"But *why?*"

She looked fiercely at me then, her face flushing so that for a moment her freckles seemed to disappear. "Why would I want to be like *you?* Why would I want to spend my whole life caring about what everybody else thinks?"

I couldn't answer her—I *did* care what people thought, although maybe I didn't care as much as someone like Deirdre did. I glimpsed myself in the mirror, looking so ordinary I was easily lost against the dull gray walls. Anna was suddenly there, reflected beside me as she leaned on her cane.

Frowning, she said, "Have a little *fun*, dear." I turned to look at her and she lifted her limp hand as if to touch my face. But it only made it as far as my elbow. She rested it there, cold against my skin. "Life's too short to be taken seriously."

I pulled away from her bony touch. "All right. Here it is, then. This is what I'd wear," I said, pulling anything off the rack. "This is my dream dress."

Anna looked delighted when I held up a sequined dress much like Elsa's, except in red. "Why, that will fit you to a T."

I did try it on, grateful for a moment to escape their scrutiny behind the bathroom door. When I came out and looked in the mirror, I didn't recognize myself.

"It's the new you!" Elsa exclaimed.

"I don't need a new me." But I hadn't known that I could ever look like that—not beautiful exactly but, well, powerful. And I felt powerful. I felt like I could swing around as Elsa had. But I didn't. I felt them watching me.

"I'll let you have it for half price," said Anna.

"That's okay."

"I'll give it to you then," said Anna pleadingly. She leaned so far forward on her cane I was afraid she'd fall.

I thought about having that dress. But I would never have Elsa's courage to wear it outside of the privacy of my own room. It would always just hang in my closet. I reached around to undo the zipper.

THIRTEEN

Now that I had met Leonard, my mother began to see him all the time. He frequently took her out to dinner, although she always came home at the end of the evening. On weekends we all did things together, like going on picnics, and Sunday afternoons my mother and I often spent at Leonard's place. I was grateful to be able to escape our apartment, where we weren't completely settled.

His house, tucked away in a densely wooded lot, wasn't anything like our old house, but I was comfortable there, charmed by its rustic feel; it felt like a cabin, with one large room and open rafters. Instead of a couch, he had a hammock that hung between two beams, and a couple of antique wooden bus-stop benches. There were two bedrooms and they were upstairs in a loft area, under the skylights. They were separated from each other only by partitions, and the doors were striped brown-and-black curtains. All the windows were lined with blue, green and brown bottles so that the sun fell through them as though through stained glass.

I don't think my mother was nearly as comfortable there; she would sit tentatively on the benches and couldn't imagine swinging in an indoor hammock. But Leonard had given her free rein of his garden, knowing how much she missed her own. One Sunday after a salmon brunch that Leonard made himself, she went out to work on the zucchini patch she was planting while I helped Leonard finish up with the dishes—my mother would have helped, but Leonard always insisted that she "relax and enjoy" herself. As he handed me a bowl to dry, he said, "I hope I'm not monopolizing you."

"What?"

"You don't seem to see much of your father. At least not on weekends."

"I see him. Besides, it's always been this way—we never really spent much time together."

"That's too bad."

"It's not like we didn't get along. We've always gotten along, sometimes better than me and my mother. It's just that . . ." I looked out at her from the window above the counter. She was wearing another old Easter hat. "I guess we could never really talk. Not about anything that didn't involve my mother anyway."

He began sponging off the counter. "You don't talk very much about things anyway, do you?"

"What . . . things?"

"You just strike me as kind of reserved." He smiled. "Maybe that's true of only children. I wouldn't know. I grew up with four brothers and sisters."

"I talk to you," I said vaguely.

"You do. But you must have been feeling a lot through all this, and it must be hard *not* having someone like a sibling to share it with. Must be kind of like . . . well, like when you're playing your guitar and you're the only one really listening."

He made me feel as exposed then as I'd thought only my mother could make me feel, and I had to look away. But something unclenched itself like a fist inside me, and for the first time since my parents had separated I didn't feel afraid. He'd been drying his hands and I reached for them where he'd folded them on his towel. "Thanks," I said, for a moment squeezing them.

He squeezed my hand back. "For what?"

I was strangely stirred by the feel of his hands, weathered and strong from all the woodworking he'd done. This so surprised and disturbed me I had to move away from him. I reached for the last dish in the drain.

"I don't know," I said, trying to sound casual. "Just thanks."

ONE SATURDAY ABOUT a month later, we were picnicking at a pond in our neighborhood. The pond was smaller than the one my mother used to take me to, but there were ducks here as well.

"Feels like we're almost in the country," said my mother, after we'd eaten. We sat on a quilt, surrounded by half-full containers.

Leonard sat leaning back against a tree. "Almost. If it weren't for all that traffic."

There was someone walking toward us. From the neon-green hoop earrings, suspenders and shoelaces, I knew it was Elsa. A little girl trailed behind her, dragging a toy plastic shopping cart. I'd forgotten that she lived directly across the park.

"Well," said my mother, when Elsa had stopped in front of us. "Don't you glow."

I hadn't mentioned Elsa to my mother or to anyone else.

Elsa grinned impishly. "Just in case you might lose me one dark stormy night."

"Oh," said my mother, looking confused.

Before I could introduce her, she announced, "I'm Elsa. And this is my sister, Audrey. Say hi, Audrey."

The little girl only stared. She'd taken a plastic steak

from the cart and now cradled it. Her mouth was rimmed with cherry so that she looked like a miniature clown.

"Hello, Audrey," said my mother, her eyes lighting up as they always did around small children. "I'm Mrs. Flynn, and this is Mr. Miller."

"Call me Leonard."

"I know who you are," said Elsa. "Leslie's told me all about you."

"Has she?" he said, sounding pleased.

"She says you make cabinets."

"And what else has Leslie told you about me?"

"That's it, basically."

He nodded, looking, I thought, a little disappointed.

"You two know each other from school?" asked my mother.

"Kind of," said Elsa, settling down beside her. Audrey sat down too. With her head pressed against Elsa's shoulder, she pushed her cart back and forth by one of the bright yellow wheels. "Actually . . ." said Elsa, pulling at the grass, "you know me."

"I do?"

"From the school parties you used to give. You gave the best parties."

"Did I? Well, thank you."

"And your birds. I remember all those birds. You used to let us touch them—that was amazing, that you trusted little kids with things like that." She looked at her sister, so much younger, and I thought how easily Elsa might be mistaken for her mother. "You would have loved those birds, wouldn't you have, Audrey?"

Audrey hugged her steak more closely.

"And what do you have in your cart?" asked my mother. "Are you planning a big family dinner?"

Audrey ran a finger back and forth inside her lower lip, only nodding.

"I hope I'm invited."

"Maybe," said Audrey, the first words she'd spoken, and I could tell that my mother had won her over just as she had won over Elsa all those years ago. But Audrey looked suddenly afraid; the ducks had wandered up from the pond.

"They're not going to hurt us," said my mother. "They've just heard we're having a picnic. And it just so happens . . ." she said, reaching for our plates, "that we have some bread crusts to share with them." Standing up, she put out her hand to Audrey. "Wouldn't you like to go say hello?"

She and Audrey started down toward the water, with Elsa following. In a moment they were surrounded by the ducks, Audrey watching in awe as they nearly took the bread right out of my mother's hand.

"I can see how your mother must have been great with kids," said Leonard.

"I'd forgotten that," I said. "How proud I used to be of her."

"You're not still proud?"

"I am. It's just different now." I was remembering the times when I'd hated her so. I hadn't been able to see this, how spontaneously she could love.

"You're a good daughter, Leslie."

I looked at him.

"You take good care of her."

"We take care of each other."

"I know. But maybe you've had to grow up a little more quickly than if your father were still here. If he were still the one taking care of things."

I watched as an ant made its way across the quilt. "Maybe."

We sat close enough for our shoulders to barely touch, and I wondered what it would feel like to lean against him. When he wasn't around, sometimes I'd catch myself thinking about him as I had only ever thought about Todd. I sat up straighter so that we weren't quite as close.

Something made me look up. Elsa was staring at us.

"Maybe it's time I stole your mother away," said Leonard, abruptly getting up.

The ducks dispersed as Leonard approached my mother. Audrey looked after my mother longingly, it seemed, as Leonard led her down to the water. Finally

Elsa was able to coax Audrey away by reminding her of her cart.

Elsa sat beside me on the quilt. "He likes you."

"What?"

"It's you he's interested in."

"How can you say that?"

"I saw how he looks at you, watches you. The only reason he's down there now is because he caught me watching him."

My mother crouched by the pond testing the water. When she stood up, she moved closer to Leonard. But he was looking in the other direction—at nothing in particular, it seemed—as he stood with his hands clasped tightly behind his back. He made no move to touch her.

I was glad when Audrey obstructed our view, overturning her cart in front of us. She held it above her head shaking it long after all the plastic food had spilled out, as if expecting one more thing, some little surprise.

I TRIED NOT to think about what Elsa had said. But I'd decided that my mother and Leonard needed more time alone. It was raining the following Saturday and Leonard offered to take us all to a movie. He was coming over early so that we'd have time for a pizza lunch, but I told my mother that I had too many exams to prepare for and had to stay home.

"Oh," she said, sounding disappointed. "Well, your grades *are* more important."

I was studying on my bed when he arrived, and I heard my mother tell him that she would be just a minute, she wasn't quite finished dressing. There was a knock at my door. Before I could answer Leonard was already poking his head in. "Hi."

"Oh, hi," I said, pretending to have been lost in my history lesson.

"Your mother says you can't come with us."

"I really have a lot of studying."

"That's too bad. It's supposed to be a great movie." He smiled. "Maybe you might actually learn something."

"I really do have to study."

"I know. I'm just giving you a hard time." I thought he'd leave then, but then he asked, "Do you mind if I come in? I've never seen your room."

"There's not much to see."

"Sure there is. You can tell a lot about a person from their room," he said, examining the pictures of New England landscapes I'd torn out from a calendar and hung on my wall. "And I can tell that you long for quiet, serene places. A place where everything makes sense."

I looked back at my history book. He understood me too easily.

He sat on the edge of my bed. "You're not avoiding me, are you?"

"Why would I be avoiding you?"

"Maybe I've said or done something to upset you, and you're not telling me about it."

I shut my book. "You haven't done anything, really. I just think you and Mom need more time alone."

He nodded, for a moment looking over at the calendar pictures. Then, looking back at me, he said, "The thing is, Leslie . . ." He put his hand on my ankle. "It's you I want to spend time with." His hand moved up along my calf, caressing it. I was wearing shorts.

I pulled my legs up to my chest.

"I'm sorry," he said hurriedly.

I looked away from him. I looked at my bureau, where there were clustered all those familiar things, my painted wooden boxes and porcelain barrette dishes.

"It's just that . . . oh, God." He rubbed his face and looked up at the ceiling. "Your mother's a charming, lovely woman. And you're all those things too. But I can't go on deceiving both you *and* your mother."

"Please leave," I said, hearing myself as if from very far away.

He got off my bed. "All right," he said, with the same gentleness he'd always used with me. On his way to the door he paused at my bureau and fingered a barrette in one of the dishes. "But you can't tell me you didn't feel something too."

"I'm ready!" said my mother, bursting in. She looked

so happy. So young. But worry creased her forehead when she looked from Leonard to me. "Have I been taking too long?"

"We should go," said Leonard, not giving her a chance to step farther into the room. In a moment they were gone.

I should probably have stopped her from going out on even one more date with him, but I could imagine how she would pull at the skin on the back of her hands; while she'd watched my father pack up all his books from his study, she had pulled as hard as if she'd hoped the physical pain would dull the pain of his leaving. I was unable to move from my bed until long after they'd left the apartment. I couldn't be alone. I needed to find Elsa.

I HAD NO real way of knowing which house was Elsa's, except that she'd once told me that hers was the only three-family house on Holt Street with a Nativity scene set up out front all year long. Their landlord, she'd said, was as lazy about putting it away after every Christmas as he was about unclogging their sinks.

Mary's face was worn away so that in the rainy shadows of the stable it shone like a pale moon. A sheep had fallen, supported now by a king. The baby was missing from the manger.

I rang the top bell, and in a moment I heard someone

running downstairs. It was Elsa, but she'd only open the door a crack. "What are you doing here?"

"I just thought you could come out for a while."

"I can't. I'm watching my sister."

"All right," I said, turning away, wondering why I was there in the first place.

"Wait a minute." She opened the door wider. "Come on up."

I was surprised at how plainly she was dressed, in sweatpants and a T-shirt, though she was just wearing them around the house.

"Take off your shoes first. My mother's just had the floors done and she's obsessive about them."

The living room floor shone like a mirror, but the room seemed empty, with only two matching plaid chairs and a coffee table. "My mother sold the couch to pay for the floors," Elsa explained. When she saw me looking at the coffee table, which was littered with cereal bowls and surrounded by seat pillows, she said, "And she sold the kitchen table to pay for having the kitchen cabinets stripped. So now we eat Japanese style in the living room." The apartment felt as bare as if they too hadn't finished unpacking.

"Come say hello to Audrey," said Elsa, carrying the bowls into the kitchen.

Audrey was playing on the checkered black-and-white linoleum floor. She sat in the middle of a large piece of brown wrapping paper, surrounded by crayons. The kitchen seemed larger without a table.

"You know what? She drew her very first house today, didn't you, Audrey? Show Leslie your house."

Audrey pointed to a corner of the paper where she'd drawn what looked like a small purple igloo.

"That's really something, Audrey," I said.

"Isn't it? I'm so *proud* of her," said Elsa, leaning down to kiss the top of her head.

"Where's your mother anyway?"

"She works Saturdays. Manages the Coaster Deli. You can have a seat anywhere, on the counter if you like. I just need to finish up with these," she said, kneading a ball of dough and placing it on a cookie sheet. I was as surprised to see her baking as I was to see her in sweatpants.

"You were right. About Leonard," I said.

"He made a pass at you, huh?"

I looked at her. "Has that happened to you?"

She nodded. "Someone right after Garry left. But that guy was a sleaze, though. Leonard . . . well, he maybe really likes you."

I pulled myself up onto the counter.

"Do you like him back?" Elsa asked.

"I told you I like him."

"I mean, are you attracted to him?"

"God, Elsa."

"Why's that so unreasonable?" She laughed. "You can feel attracted to him without actually sleeping with him—"

"He's going out with my *mother*."

Elsa thoughtfully ran her finger around the batter bowl before dumping it into the sink.

"I wasn't thinking about me. I was thinking about my mother. I wanted it to work out for them. And I thought it was working out . . . I don't know. Maybe I wanted it to work out too much."

"What did you expect? For them to marry?"

"My mother needs to be married."

"Nobody *needs* to be married. Marriage is a ridiculous institution anyway, don't you know that by now?" she said, noisily sliding the tray into the oven and slamming shut the door. "What is the point of vows if you can break them? It's like you're only pretending, playing house. The only real thing is when they leave."

I looked at her, taken aback by her anger. "Like your father left?"

"My father *died*."

A woman came in and dumped a couple of bags on the counter beside me. "Well, who's this?" she asked. Her hair was the same red as Elsa's but she wore it flipped back like I wore mine. She could have easily blended in with the girls at school.

"Leslie, this is my mother," said Elsa, not looking

at us as she crouched to hand Audrey the spatula to lick.

"What a surprise," her mother said. "Elsa never has anyone over." She seemed to be wearing a mask, her freckles barely showing beneath her foundation. On her way to the refrigerator she let one hand brush the top of Audrey's head. "And how's my little one?"

"She drew her first house today," said Elsa.

"That's *terrific*," she said, opening a can of diet Coke. "I'm starved. Oh, and your cookies smell so good." She looked at me, patting one hip. "If it weren't for Elsa, I wouldn't be so fat. Oh, wait till you see . . ." she said, pulling a thin box out from one of her shopping bags. Inside the box was a pair of men's leather gloves.

"What does he need those for?" asked Elsa.

"It's our anniversary—we've been together six months now."

"Happy anniversary," said Elsa flatly. "So what are you going to sell to pay for those?"

"Don't be nasty, Elsa. They were on sale."

"Even leather gloves on sale can't be a good deal."

Her mother seemed about to say something but merely slipped on one of the gloves. She held out her hand admiringly.

Elsa looked at her. "You didn't pay for those, did you?"

"They're just *gloves*, Elsa. Don't carry on so."

"Shit, Mom."

"You know how I hate that kind of language around Audrey."

"I don't care. You haven't done that in a while. Why are you starting again?"

Elsa's mother threw the gloves back into their box and, looking at me, said, "What is it, anyway, with your generation? We're being poisoned by carbon monoxide, can destroy the earth how many times over, and you all worry about a pair of gloves? Where's your sense of perspective?" She grabbed up the rest of her bags. As she left the kitchen, she added, "I know you don't like Tony, Elsa, and I'm sorry about that. But he's still around, isn't he?"

We listened to her heels clattering across the bare floors, until there was the sound of a television being turned on.

Elsa slid down to the floor so that she was leaning against the cabinets. "She hasn't done that for a while."

I slid down beside her. "Shoplifting?"

"She used to pick little things off store shelves like lipsticks, things like that. I remember admiring her, how swift she was. Or at least I admired her until she started taking bigger things, like cosmetic cases and alarm clocks." She was quiet for a moment, then, gazing at Audrey, said, "Look at her. Look at how I've taught her things, like how to love herself."

"To love herself?"

"Sure. Look how she hardly knows we're here."

Audrey had abandoned the spatula, having discovered her sneakers that lay near her on the floor. She had pulled out one lace and was relacing it her own way. She seemed entirely absorbed, and I supposed that's what Elsa meant by loving herself. But against the empty checkered floor she seemed left behind somehow, and I was reminded of her as she'd been at the park—wavering unsteadily as she'd stood there gazing after my mother.

"Do you remember your father?" I asked.

"Remember him?" She looked at me incredulously it seemed, then gazed back at Audrey. "I have images of him. But then I'm not so sure how much I'm remembering, how much is photographs—pictures we haven't looked at in years." Elsa sat with her legs sprawled and seemed now to be gazing at her toe which she wriggled through a hole in her sock. "It's been so long. It surprises me sometimes that I still love him."

She seemed so much like a child then, her plans for building her own boat and sailing around the world probably really were no more than dreams. I was as disappointed as I had been when I'd first seen her at the door looking so ordinary. As disappointed as I'd been in myself when I hadn't bought that dress. But we were perhaps more alike than I'd imagined, and I couldn't decide whether I was relieved or frightened by that. I only knew that I felt oddly at home there, in an apartment that felt as unsettled and transitory as our own. The oven bell rang and I stayed there for a while longer, nibbling on her cookies and playing with Audrey. I didn't know what I was going to tell my mother.

SHE WAS ALREADY home when I got back, sitting in the chair my father had always sat in. She had a prayer book face down on her lap as she stared at the wall. I wasn't used to her sitting so still, without even her hands moving. The light flooded the room like ice melting.

When she saw me, she didn't try to hide that pinched look. "He told me he couldn't see me anymore," she said, "that he didn't think it would work."

I knelt beside her. "Mom."

"Just out of the blue. We went for pizza like we had planned and . . . we never even made it to the movie."

"Mom . . . it just didn't work out. You'll find someone else."

She didn't say anything, only stared down at her prayer book.

"You will. You just . . . you need to get over Daddy."

She started to cry then. Since my father had left, I'd hear her cry when she was alone in her room, crying into her pillow so that I wouldn't hear her. She'd never before cried in front of me.

"We'll be fine, Mom, really."

She looked at me.

"We'll be okay."

She searched my face like she used to, but without cupping my chin, without touching me. Shaking her head, she said quietly, "You're all grown up, aren't you?"

Something felt different between us, as it had that night when we'd sat together on the steps in our old house, when for a moment we seemed to have become like friends. Now, with my mother looking at me so intensely, we seemed to have become more than that; we'd become two women capable of attracting and being attracted to the same man. That we could possibly have arrived at that same point seemed unimaginable, the real reason why I hadn't been able to admit to Elsa about actually having been attracted to my own mother's boyfriend.

I found myself wanting her to hold me, to surround me like she used to. But I got up, saying, "Come on. We need to finish unpacking."

She leaned back tiredly. "Now?"

I put out my hand to help her out of the chair. "We're going to be here for a while."

WE NEVER HEARD from Leonard again. He even stopped coming into the bookstore. But we did finish unpacking that day, even my mother's bird collection. She arranged the sea gulls on the fake mantel and the pelicans, that had framed our old front stoop, on our deck overlooking the parking lot. Elsa came over with Audrey, who fell in love with the plastic owl clock whose eyes shifted back and forth. Of all her birds, my mother liked this one the least, a present from Aunt Holly. But I could tell that she was immensely pleased; she didn't mind Audrey asking her to take the clock right off the wall so that she could touch it. She allowed Audrey to touch all her birds as she'd allowed us when we were small. People didn't always admire her birds. Sometimes they didn't notice them at all.

FOURTEEN

Those things that had begun to feel so different between my mother and me became our anchor; there were more and more moments when we found ourselves just sitting together, sometimes out on the porch where she had planted a trumpet vine to wind around the railing, or at the table, when occasionally we were both still up nights, drinking hot chocolate. We hadn't exactly become good friends, at least not in the way that Aunt Holly and Meg had been friends—I don't think we would ever really be able to talk openly enough for that. What we had now was more of an allegiance; we were two women faced with having no alternative but to redefine ourselves.

After Leonard, I don't think my mother stopped

hoping to find someone, she just stopped expecting to. She was the last person who'd want to end up living her life alone, but she seemed to be preparing herself for it anyway; she'd often spend her evenings sitting in the living room as she had the night Leonard broke up with her, and sometimes she would not even have a prayer book in her lap. Her hands would rest motionless on the arms of the chair, except for maybe one finger that gently picked at the knotty fabric. She would sit as still as if she were testing out this new aloneness, trying to feel how comfortably it could fit.

I didn't meet anyone else that I could like as much as Todd, or even Leonard, but that was all right. Like my mother, I hadn't stopped hoping to find someone. I just didn't feel as pressed to find that someone while I was in high school. My choice not to sleep with Chip had been the beginning of larger choices, all of which had to do not with what was expected of me but with what made me feel most whole—I'd begun to develop my own dreams, although not ones as abstract as Elsa's. I was already thinking more seriously about going on to law school after college.

WHEN IT CAME time for me to go to college, my father was supposed to drive me up. But a couple of weeks after my graduation he and Clarkson moved to New Mexico, where Clarkson was to begin research on the

Pueblo Indians. He'd taken a teaching position at the University of Albuquerque. They'd bought a place together there, even though he'd told me that he didn't intend to marry Clarkson. He never wanted to marry again. Clarkson wasn't interested in marrying either, since her research work would always have to come first. They got along so well, he said, because they were able to "enjoy each other unconditionally."

He sent me pictures of their adobe house. There was sand and scrub bushes in their yard instead of trees. In one picture the two of them are sitting on the ledge of their stone fireplace. He has his arm around her and her hand rests on his thigh. There's a huge turquoise ring on her index finger and he wears a turquoise clasp on one of those rope ties I imagined only ranchers wore. He doesn't look like himself, as if he were acting in a play. But he looks entirely happy, leaning his head against hers and smiling broadly. Proudly. It hurt to see him so happy. Happier than he'd even looked with my mother. He'd asked me to visit them over my January break so that the three of us could drive up to the mountains. I said I'd think about it.

IT WAS MY mother who finally had to drive me up to Cornell. "Everyone's climbing up my back," she said, as she sat hunched over the wheel squinting through the windshield as if it were raining in torrents. It was a clear September day.

"Just relax," I said, "and mind your own business. They can pass if they want. Just go whatever speed you're comfortable with."

Driving on expressways had always terrified my mother, but she had to practice for her drive back alone that afternoon. She wouldn't spend the night in a motel; she'd never slept well in a strange bed. That summer we'd practiced on the expressways going back and forth from my grandparents' house. Since she was working full-time now at the bookstore, we'd only been able to go out there on weekends. My grandmother kept pinned on her refrigerator the "parables" that Grampa Cole had drawn at the center he now attended for the memory impaired. They weren't parables that made any sense— a horse looking at a dog, the dog looking at a cat and the cat looking at an apple so that "the horse wouldn't think that he was dirty." But he was being treated by trained specialists and the drawings were meant to exercise his mind. They were drawn shakily, and I could imagine Grampa Cole's red hands, cold and swollen now from bad circulation, moving slowly and deliberately across the page. Sometimes after Gramma June had shut the refrigerator she'd run her hand over a drawing, over the little animals, as if she could actually feel some texture in his pen strokes, some soothing woolly kind of softness. He didn't always know her anymore. He didn't always recognize any of us anymore.

Sweat glistened on my mother's forehead even

though there was a cool breeze blowing through the car. She craned her head so far out over the wheel I could see the muscles straining in her neck.

"You hungry?" I asked.

She seemed to relax at just the mention of her picnic, leaning back a little and stretching her fingers. "Yes, I think I could eat."

"EVERYONE'S IN SUCH a hurry," she sighed, getting out of the car after we'd pulled over. Her white blouse was soaked through so that I could see her bra straps. She'd taken off her bluish-gray jacket and the rumpled matching skirt clung to her thighs. She'd bought the suit especially for this day. She rarely wore such dark colors and never a suit, but she had been determined to look "sophisticated" for me, hoping to look like she'd gone to college when she hadn't. The only note of color was the pink hat pin in her dark blue beret.

We sat beneath a pine tree that rained down its needles on us. She knelt on the quilt I'd spread out and gazed into the picnic basket. The thought of unpacking all that food seemed to exhaust her.

"You were great, Mom."

She looked at me. "Do you really think so?"

"Yeah. You were nervous, but you didn't let that get in the way of your driving. You really kept your cool."

Smiling, she reached into the basket and began unloading the containers. "I *was* nervous."

"So was I the first few times."

"Maybe. But you've got your father's calm collect-edness." She examined the carrot cake she'd made, gently pressing in the sides where it had begun to crumble. "You're a lot like him. In a good way, that is."

It wasn't often that my mother alluded to my father as being anything *but* good. She would never be convinced that my father's leaving had been anything but entirely her fault.

"And what would be a bad way?" I asked.

She became flustered, dropping the napkins. Scrambling after them, she said, "Well, not bad actually. Just not . . . just that you're able to see that there might be another side to things. That's all." For a moment she folded her hands on top of the napkins. She stared out at the traffic as she would stare at our living room wall. "But your father meant well. He always meant well."

EXCEPT FOR WHEN my mother ran into my father at the cleaners and they were meeting with their lawyers to make the final divorce arrangements, she had seen my father only twice since they'd separated. The first time had been when we were selling the house, and he came over to help clean out the garage. She hid inside, watching him from behind the dining room curtain. I hoped he wouldn't see her there as I helped him bag old paint cans and deflated beach balls I'd forgotten about. He was testing out the hand mower, the blades long since rusted, when she ran out and pleaded with him to come back. She kept trying to embrace him and he had to shake her off. Finally he got into his car, telling me that he would come back later once she'd calmed down.

The second time she saw him was at my high school graduation. I was glad that he hadn't brought Clarkson. The ceremony took place on the football field, and when my mother's heels caught in the Astroturf, she let him support her by one elbow. She seemed to have finally accepted that they would never get back together, but she had trouble looking at him whenever he spoke; she would shade her eyes and scan the crowd as if looking for someone she knew. I'd begun to worry then that she'd never be able to stop loving my father.

At the same time, she seemed to draw strength from that love as she did from her prayers. She seemed to be most inspired by what she could not have in life, what ultimately was as remote as the Holy Spirit; she'd never had the close friends she'd always hoped for, but neither had she ever really tried for them. When she once had, it was with an eighty-nine-year-old woman whose friendship couldn't have lasted for very long anyway. And she'd always been unhappy living in New Jersey, complaining about the lack of "open spaces" for as far back as I could remember. Now that there was nothing to keep her there, she'd decided to stay, and planned to have our living room wallpapered. If she ever found herself with all those things she'd missed most in life, her capacity to love might completely dry up. And for so many years her love for me and my father had threatened to consume us. But what I now could see more clearly than my father had ever been able to was that her love, when allowed to rest like a great lion in the shade of a tree, could be peaceably admired for its beauty.

It seemed to take my mother forever to unpack all the containers. I'd been waiting so long for this day I just wanted to get there. That summer, I'd worked as a stock girl in a drugstore, and while replenishing the greeting card racks I'd wonder about the new friends I'd make at Cornell, what my roommate, Julie Sullivan, would be like—I knew her name from the orientation book they'd sent me. Elsa hadn't applied to college. She just wanted to get her own place, imagining a sunny kitchen with cats curled on the counters. She'd taken to drawing houses she'd like to build instead of boats, houses with tall columns and curving stairways, houses you could become lost in.

"WE SHOULD BE going soon, I suppose," my mother said, after we'd eaten as much as we could. But then she took off her shoes and stretched out her legs, crossing them at the ankles. "Is there anything we forgot to pack for you? What about those sweaters I left drying in the bathroom, did you get those?"

"I did."

"And your snow boots. Oh, your boots, I'm sure we forgot those. I know because they're tucked way in the back of the hall closet."

"I can get them some weekend."

She looked at me blankly.

"I *will* be coming home," I laughed.

"I know. I know you will." She spread out her fingers across the quilt. "But you don't have to. You don't have to come home if you don't want to."

"I want to."

She gathered the quilt into her fist.

I leaned over to kiss her. "Really."

Her eyes suddenly filled, their olive green brightening. "What have I ever done . . ."

I picked off the pine needles that had fallen into her lap. "Did you bring any seed?"

She wiped one finger under each eye, then rummaged through the bottom of the basket. "You poor little things, you've been waiting so patiently," she said to the sparrows fluttering along the edge of the trees.

"Do you want me to drive the rest of the way?" I asked.

"Oh." She looked back at the traffic as if she'd forgotten about it. "No. No, that's all right." She forced a smile. "I'll be fine."

———

AN UPPERCLASSMAN HELPED me up with my duffel bags and trunk. Julie Sullivan hadn't arrived yet. The room was small, but so starkly furnished it felt large and drafty. There were just two of everything, two desks, two beds and two bureaus. The walls were a brownish yellow.

I sat on one of the beds and looked toward the windows. A thin cloud brushed past a tree before passing out of sight. The voices from outside and the sound of car doors slamming sounded very far away, as if we were much higher up than the second floor. The bottom of my stomach seemed to drop out. I longed suddenly to lie down and go to sleep.

My mother sat next to me. She pressed her hand into the mattress. "How nice and firm."

I couldn't look away from the window, afraid that I would cry; I was already missing her. I was missing her as I could miss Grampa Cole when he was right there beside me eating dinner at my grandparents' porch table. He'd ask me why I no longer brought him presents of calico kittens hidden in one of my mother's old handbags, confusing me with a little girl he used to play with back in Maine. They'd make the kittens climb the ladders of his toy fire engines up in his room.

I felt the light touch of my mother's fingers on my back. "It will look a little more cheerful once we unpack a little."

I nodded.

She got up and looked in the mirror above one of the bureaus, pulling out her pin to fix her hat. "Oh, dear," she sighed, taking out her compact to powder her nose. She shook her head as if there were nothing she could do to make herself look better.

"Hi!" a girl boomed cheerfully from the doorway. "I'm Julie Sullivan."

"I'm Leslie Flynn," I croaked, my voice suddenly gone.

She wore her short blond hair back in a red terry cloth headband that matched her red Lacoste shirt, a tiny green alligator stitched to one breast. She pulled in a large brown suitcase on wheels, followed by her father who pulled in an identical suitcase. Her mother carried a hockey stick, a tennis racket and an assortment of small bags, one of which must have been a cosmetic case. Four brothers and sisters filed in, each carrying something, even a red beanbag chair. A boy of about ten flopped into the chair. He spun a Frisbee on one finger. The room was as suddenly filled as if everyone had arrived for a party at once.

"She's our first to fly the coop," said her father, holding Julie in front of him as if posing for a picture.

"Yes, well," said my mother, "Leslie too." I tried to ignore how they all stared at her, how awkward and stiff she seemed in her suit. Her shyness getting the best of her, she bent to pull out the sheets from the bottom of my duffel.

I wished then that my father were there—he had always been good with large groups of people. But they all seemed very interested in me, wanting to know where I was from, even what kind of music I liked. Julie liked jazz but she'd send her records right back home if I didn't. I laughed, warmed by her earnestness. I showed her the poster of Degas' dancers that my mother had given me. She said that she loved it, even though her own posters were of puppies and raccoons hanging from tree limbs.

I'd forgotten about my mother until she tapped me on the shoulder. Not only had she made my bed, but she'd propped up my stuffed panda on my pillow, which now embarrassed me. She'd even unpacked my shampoos and makeup, organizing them into the heart-shaped plastic baskets she'd bought for me to keep on my bureau.

"I think I should be going now," she said, "if I don't want to get caught in the dark."

"Oh," I said, looking at my watch. "I'll walk down with you then."

"No," she exclaimed. Then, more quietly, she said, "Really. I'll just go." Without really looking at them, she briefly waved good-bye to the Sullivans.

I walked with her to the stairs. She took my head

between her hands, looking at me as if she were about to say something important. Instead, she began rattling on about fabric softener. "You'll notice I tucked a little bottle of it in, and it's now on your top shelf in the closet, with your shoe polish. Don't forget to put it in with your laundry, especially your sheets. They're brand-new and I've already washed them once, but it will take a few more washings to soften them. And with a little softener in them, I think you'll sleep better, you know how you've always had sensitive skin—" She stopped as if to catch her breath before going on, but only said, "You'll forget anyway, won't you?"

I smiled. "Probably."

She hugged me so hard then, but in a second was already letting me go. "Good-bye, sweetheart." In the next moment she had turned the corner on the landing, her heels clicking rapidly, frantically it seemed, down the stairs.

"Drive carefully!" I called.

I watched her from the landing window. She nearly ran to the car, holding onto her hat. The way she rushed so, I expected her to jerk out of her parking spot and hit someone. Instead, she took a long time backing out. As she drove away, I could see how she was hunched back over the steering wheel and I found myself praying. Rather, I fell into a kind of prayer as I used to fall gently forward into the water when I'd wade out into Indian

Lake. I fell into it as easily as I thought my mother always had. But I was praying for nothing in particular, only for God to be somewhere nearby, for something, anything at all, to be watching over me and my mother now.

Books in the
HARVEST AMERICAN WRITING SERIES

The Choiring of the Trees
Donald Harington

Let the Dead Bury Their Dead
Randall Kenan

Patchwork
Karen Osborn

Marbles
Oxford Stroud

Blue Glass
Sandra Tyler